ROOT NOTES

by

Deep Menon

Copyright © 2025 Pradeep Premalatha Venugopal

All rights reserved

The characters and events portrayed in this book are fictitious. Any similarity to real persons, living or dead, is coincidental and not intended by the author.

No part of this book may be reproduced, or stored in a retrieval system, or transmitted in any form or by any means, electronic, mechanical, photocopying, recording, or otherwise, without express written permission of the publisher.

ISBN: 9798308525714

Cover design by: Art Painter
Library of Congress Control Number: 2018675309
Printed in the United States of America

Dedicated to My Daughter

To my beloved daughter, whose bright eyes and steadfast heart remind me daily that the world still has room for wonder:

This book was born of simple moments those quiet dawn hours under a generous tree, and the hush of a village that knows both hardship and hope. It began with a child's gentle spirit, curious about everything yet certain of nothing. In the space between her questions and the old stories whispered by elders, I recognized a theme that echoes across every land: innocence is a treasure, often overlooked, always in danger of slipping away.

The story that follows paints a place where the ancient and the modern collide, where the laughter of children competes with the demands of an unrelenting world. Through the eyes of young Naledi, we glimpse how easily that sense of pure-hearted wonder can be threatened by the machinery of "progress." And yet, in her every heartbeat, we see the proof that each of us carries a spark of curiosity and kindness—if only we dare to protect it.

I offer these pages to you, my daughter, in the hope that you will carry forward the joy of asking "why", the courage to dream "how", and the determination to stand by what feels right, even when the world claims it's easier to let go. May you always pause to listen to the quiet creak of branches overhead, the hush of morning light, and the whispers of your own heart. For if we cherish the simple wonders and guard them against the noise of a hurried age, we may yet preserve the innocence that enriches us all.

May this tale remind you and every reader of what is worth holding onto when the rest of the world insists we move on too quickly. And above all, may you never lose the gentle strength that comes from believing in the unspoken magic around us.

DEEP MENON

UNDER LEAF AND LIGHT

If you happened upon Naledi's village at daybreak, you'd find twelve huts huddled together on a dusty plain, their thatched roofs catching the first blush of the rising sun. At that hour, not much stirs save for a rooster or two, bold enough to announce the morning, and perhaps a donkey complaining about a load far too heavy for dawn. Yet if you wandered just a stone's throw beyond those huts, your eye would be caught by something mighty hard to miss: a towering, ancient tree that seems to cradle the horizon in its outstretched limbs.

They call it the Great Tree, and for good reason. Its trunk is thick as two grown men standing side by side, the bark knotted and furrowed like the face of a wise old grandmother. Its canopy spreads wide enough to shade half the village by midday if the sun's high and the weather kindly. Some folks say the tree is older than memory itself; others claim it was planted by a legendary ancestor. Naledi, at just ten years old, hasn't made up her mind which tale rings true; she only knows she can't stay away from it.

Come the hush of dawn, you'd likely find Naledi right here: a thin, barefoot child with eyes shining in the first glow of morning. She stands beneath the sprawling branches, toes pressed into the rough earth, her small hand resting gently against the trunk. From a distance, you might think she's listening for a heartbeat or a secret voice. And in a sense, you'd be right.

"Mama says I daydream too much," Naledi murmurs, turning her face upward as though the Great Tree might speak. A light breeze stirs the leaves, creating a faint rustle that might pass for a greeting. "But I can't help it," she goes on, her words just above a whisper. "I feel… I don't know… like there's something in you that wants to speak."

Of course, the tree offers no reply in any language a person could understand. Naledi waits another moment, savoring the hush of early morning. It feels like a secret world;just her, the tree, and the sense that, if she stands still enough, something magical might take root in her heart.

Suddenly, a voice calls through the stillness: "Naledi! Child, where'd you go?" It's a woman's voice, heavy with both worry and weariness;the way a mother sounds when chores outweigh the time to do them in.

Naledi sighs, giving the tree one last, longing glance. "Coming, Mama!" she shouts, dodging around the tree's exposed roots and hurrying back toward the huts.

By now, the village has fully awakened. A gray-bearded neighbor shuffles past, a yoke balanced on his shoulders with buckets of water sloshing at every step. Two children chase each other around a goat pen, giggling in the rising dust. And from a particular hut;the one leaning a touch to the left;comes the mouthwatering smell of fried dough and warm spices.

That leaning hut belongs to Naledi's family. Outside stands Zanele, her mother, tall and sinewy, dressed in a well-worn wrap. She's wiping her hands on an apron that bears the stains of flour, oil, and a thousand meals. A small wooden table in front overflows with freshly fried snacks, steam curling in the cool air.

Zanele greets Naledi with a mild frown that doesn't quite hide the affection in her eyes. "Up before the sun again, eh? Off dreaming under that old tree?" She shakes her head, but a flicker of a smile tugs at her lips. "We've got work to do, you know."

Naledi bows her head slightly, a pang of guilt prickling. "Yes, Mama, I know." She notices the steaming goodies;fried maize cakes dusted lightly with chili and salt;and her stomach rumbles its approval.

Zanele notices. "All right," she says, nudging the tray toward Naledi. "Take one. But don't go gobbling them all, or there'll be nothing left to sell at the market."

Naledi snatches a small cake and grins. "Thank you," she says, her teeth sinking into the crisp exterior and finding a warm, soft middle. For a moment, the world distills to just her and that savory mouthful;proof that sometimes, a simple bit of food can carry the promise of a whole morning.

But Zanele, practical as always, doesn't allow any delay. "Fetch me some water," she instructs. "I need to wash these bowls if we're to make more dough later."

Before Naledi can answer, another voice;deep and insistent;carries from inside the hut. "The roof's still leaking," it says. Out steps Boikonyo, her older brother, sturdy and broad for sixteen, with arms that speak of daily labor. "What's the plan, Mama? Snacks won't fix a sagging thatch."

Zanele turns, her voice patient but firm. "I know, Boikonyo. But I can't mend a roof by myself, and you've been off hauling crates for half the village."

He crosses his arms. "I have to earn money. If I don't, we'll be in worse shape."

Naledi, standing by the table, feels his words like small pebbles thrown in her direction;reminders that she's only a child, her hands more apt to daydream than repair anything. She hunches her shoulders, wishing she could disappear.

Zanele keeps her composure. "We appreciate your labor, son, but I've got to provide, too. Selling these snacks matters. And Naledi helps where she can."

Boikonyo casts Naledi a pointed look. "Helps by gazing at that tree all day," he mutters.

Naledi's cheeks burn, and she opens her mouth to argue;she does chores, too! But words tangle on her tongue. The best she can do is force out a quiet, "I do my tasks."

Zanele rests a hand on Boikonyo's arm to forestall further bickering. "Enough. Let's not start. Naledi, go get the water. We'll talk about the roof later."

Grateful for the excuse to leave, Naledi darts off around the hut, clay pitcher in hand. She hears her brother grumble something about dreamers, but chooses not to dwell on it. She passes a line of tiny vegetable plots, making her way to the communal well.

Halfway there, she greets Mama Lindiwe, perched on a stool weaving a basket from dried reeds. The elderly woman nods sagely at Naledi. "Morning, little star. Going for water?"

Naledi nods. "Yes, ma'am," she replies, pausing a moment. Memory stirs of Mama Lindiwe's tales that old trees hold the land's memories in their roots. "Mama Lindiwe, do you really think our Great Tree… remembers things?"

The old woman's eyes gleam with a quiet wisdom. She pats Naledi's arm gently. "Oh, I do, child. A tree that old has seen so much;heard our joys, our tears, our songs. Could be that's why it stands so tall: to keep those memories safe."

Naledi's heart quickens at the thought that someone else understands her bond with the tree. "That's how it feels to me," she whispers, then offers a polite farewell before continuing on.

The well is little more than a ring of stones around a dark hole, but it echoes with the splash of water below. Naledi lowers the bucket, winding it up again with effort until it emerges brimming with cool, clear water. She transfers some into her clay pitcher, careful not to spill. Balancing it against her hip, she heads back toward the hut, the weight of chores replaced by a thrill of quiet hope.

At the hut, Boikonyo is nowhere to be seen, likely off to earn his day's wages. Zanele kneads dough at a small wooden table, her brow furrowed in concentration. But the tension on her face eases a fraction when she sees Naledi return with the water. "Thank you, my child. Set it by the stove. We'll need it soon."

Naledi does so, placing the pitcher carefully to avoid spills. "Mama," she says, voice soft. "Should I help with the snack stall later?"

Zanele glances at her, a fondness flickering in her eyes. "Not tonight. Your brother insisted on standing guard at the stall, says trouble's been brewing among travelers. But I'll need you for errands in the morning."

Naledi nods, a small surge of relief mingling with curiosity about what the evening might hold. Maybe she'll steal a minute under the Great Tree, or talk to Mama Lindiwe about how, exactly, trees remember. But daily life in the village rarely stands still, so she braces herself for whatever tasks emerge.

From inside the hut, the warm smell of dough frying in the pan beckons. Zanele pulls out a fresh batch of maize cakes. Naledi takes one, the crunch of the first bite reminding her that, for all her father's unspoken dreams, for all the Great Tree's silent mysteries, there's a satisfying simplicity to a well-cooked meal.

Yet even amid this everyday bustle, she feels a gentle tug drawing her back toward the tree. A sense that it;and perhaps her father's memory;still has more to share. She pictures the broad trunk, the dusty patch where she stands to listen, and she knows that, once chores are done, her bare feet will lead her back under those ancient branches. Perhaps the tree will only offer its familiar hush, or maybe, just maybe, she'll sense that hidden, whispered call to dream big, even in a small place.

After all, she thinks, balancing the plate of steaming snacks in her arms, the tree was here before she was born and will stand long after she's gone. But right now, in this time and place, Naledi can't help believing that, if she listens closely enough, the Great Tree might reveal a tune meant just for her.

HANDS THAT STEADY, HEARTS THAT YEARN

The sun had climbed higher by the time Naledi set aside her broom, letting out a small huff of relief. She leaned it against the hut's clay wall, wiping sweat from her forehead with the back of her hand. The yard was tidy enough now ; she'd swept away the bits of straw and fallen leaves that had gathered overnight, forming a neat little pile at the far edge near a modest patch of kale and onions. Across the village, other families were stirring in earnest, chasing after goats or scolding children who were still rubbing sleep from their eyes.

But in Naledi's own yard, her mother Zanele stood at the wooden table with all the composure of a seasoned general. Several woven baskets of fried maize cakes lined the tabletop, their warm, savory smell luring a few stray chickens closer. Zanele glanced up from a small ledger book ; just a few loose sheets of paper clamped together ; and caught Naledi's eye.

"There you are," she said, sounding both relieved and a bit distracted. She patted the ledger with her fingertips. "I'm trying to make sense of these sales figures. We ran out of fritters last night, which is good, but I can't see how it all adds up exactly. Did Boikonyo put down the right amounts?"

Naledi stepped nearer, peering at the shaky handwriting

scrawled across the pages. Boikonyo's script was far from pretty ; he wrote the way a horse might plow a field if it only half cared about straight lines. "Maybe," she offered gently, picking up the pencil lying across the ledger. "It looks like he wrote four customers for the evening, but the coins in the little tin jar seemed more than that."

Zanele let out a sigh that might have been frustration if it weren't wrapped up in so much affection. "He's a good boy," she said. "But he's got a head for carrying water buckets, not for counting coins."

Naledi nodded. She could recall Boikonyo's scowl whenever he had to write more than a few words. Numbers were even worse ; each digit looked like a guess more than a fact. "I can help, Mama," she offered, gingerly taking the ledger into her hands. "I'm not perfect at math, but I can do the sums from last night. Niya's the real genius with numbers, though. She helped me with homework a few times."

Zanele smiled. "You're a blessing, child." She pushed a small pouch of coins across the table. "Go on, count these while I get today's dough ready."

Naledi slipped onto a low wooden stool and spread out the coins in neat rows. They weren't many, mostly coppers and a few tarnished silvers. She started grouping them into piles, adding up their value, marking each total in the ledger. Meanwhile, Zanele busied herself with mixing more dough ; her arms moving in a steady, practiced rhythm, her eyes occasionally drifting to watch Naledi work.

The yard was uncommonly calm for a moment: a mother and daughter, each absorbed in her tasks, the aroma of dough and spices swirling through the air. Over by the patch of kale, the stray chickens lost interest and wandered off, clucking to one another about some new discovery in the dust. But all that quiet was soon broken by the heavy tread of footsteps.

Boikonyo appeared at the entrance to the yard, carrying a bundle of dried reeds slung over one shoulder. "Found these near the river," he declared, dropping them next to the hut with a dull thump. "We can use them for patching the roof, if we ever get around to it."

Zanele paused her mixing. "Thank you," she said, eyeing the bundle. "We'll manage. But today's a market day; I have to focus on the snacks first." She didn't say more, but Naledi felt the tension in the air ; her mother was caught between needing to sell for income and wanting to placate Boikonyo's worries about the house.

He raked a hand through his short hair. "We can't keep putting it off," he warned, voice dropping to a lower register. "All it takes is one big rain, and we'll have water pouring in on our heads."

"I know," Zanele replied, gentler this time. "But we still need to earn money to buy more nails and a few planks of wood. If we just use reeds, the roof might hold for a while, but it'll collapse again come next season."

Her words hung in the air. Boikonyo's face tightened, yet he offered no further protest. Instead, he nodded curtly, as though filing the conversation away for another day. He glanced at Naledi's small coin piles. "That all we made last night?"

Naledi nodded. "I'm just adding it up. Looks like we did better than the last market day."

"Huh," Boikonyo grunted. "Well, better than nothing."

With that, he headed inside the hut, presumably to see if any morning tea remained. Zanele took a breath, then continued kneading the dough, her hands moving in that steady, methodical way that spoke of years of practice. Naledi turned back to her coin counting, but her mind wandered to the Great Tree ; she wondered if it would be too childish to ask to slip away, even for a moment. The morning sun glinted through the yard, promising that the day would only grow hotter. Perhaps a midday respite under that wide canopy could be a reward after finishing all her tasks.

"Mama," she began tentatively, as Zanele reached for more flour, "do you need me after I'm done with the coins? I was thinking, maybe I could go see Niya or Mandla for a bit. We've been talking about fixing old scraps and selling them, you know, so we can earn a little extra."

Zanele's arms paused mid-knead. "Fixing scraps?"

"Yes, Mama." Naledi's voice grew more confident. "Niya and Mandla have this idea ; like a small business. They take broken pots, pans, or tools and make them usable again. Mandla's real handy, and Niya's good with numbers. I could help gather items or talk to neighbors about what they might need repaired."

A small smile tugged at Zanele's lips. "My, my. You three are full of dreams," she said, but there was no disapproval in her tone. Quite the opposite. "If it helps the neighbors and earns a coin or two, I can't see the harm. But" ; she raised a flour-dusted finger ; "finish with those coins first. Then maybe help me pack up the snacks for the day. After that, if time allows, go on and see your friends. Just be back before late afternoon."

Naledi's heart leapt. "Thank you, Mama!" she said, grateful that her mother valued a bit of enterprise over idle daydreams. Truth be told, though, a spark of daydream lay at the root of everything Naledi did. Even as she finished summing up the coins, she pictured Mandla hammering away at a broken tin plate, Niya carefully counting out the money. Maybe Naledi's role was smaller ; just encouraging them and talking to neighbors ; but it felt good to be part of something that might help her family pay for that roof.

At last, the coins were tallied. Naledi scribbled the final figure in the ledger and carried both the pouch and the little book to Zanele. Her mother scanned the neat columns Naledi had made and gave an approving nod. "You're a natural," she murmured, slipping the ledger into a cloth bag she'd hang from her shoulder at the market. "Now let's get these cakes packed, and we'll be set."

They worked side by side, layering the fried cakes in baskets lined with cloth, making sure they wouldn't lose too much heat on the walk to the market area. Zanele also tucked in a few sweet fritters she'd experimented with, drizzled in a sugary syrup. She gave Naledi one to taste, and the girl's eyes widened at the burst of sweetness. "Mmm, that's good," she murmured, licking a spot of syrup from her thumb.

Zanele laughed. "Let's hope the customers think so too. If these sell, we might have a new favorite on our hands."

When everything was prepared, Zanele hoisted a covered basket onto her hip. "Stay here a moment," she told Naledi, "and watch the rest of the dough. I need to see if Boikonyo's coming to help or not."

Naledi nodded. She was alone in the yard, and she could hear distant chatter from a neighbor's yard, the clatter of pots or pans. A bird hopped along the top of the hut's roof, tilting its head curiously at the basket below. Naledi waved it away with a gentle hush, not wanting to lose any precious fritters to a sneaky beak.

Moments later, Boikonyo emerged from the hut, Zanele trailing behind him. He looked a touch less grumpy than before ; probably the effect of having had a cup of tea. "All right," he said. "I'll carry one of the baskets. Let's see how much we can sell this morning."

Naledi straightened up. "Are you both going to the market now?"

Zanele nodded. "We want to catch the early crowd ; day workers who might pass through before heading out to the fields or the next village over. You can stay here, look after the dough, and keep an eye on the yard. If you finish everything, you can go see

Niya and Mandla. But remember, watch that pot on the stove in a bit. The oil's still cooling, and we don't want anything catching fire."

"Yes, Mama," Naledi replied dutifully, already feeling a swirl of excitement in her stomach at the thought of visiting her friends.

Boikonyo scooped up another basket, balancing it carefully, and he and Zanele set off. Naledi watched them go, noticing the firm set of Boikonyo's shoulders and the determined line of Zanele's jaw. They both carried burdens ; literal and figurative ; and Naledi couldn't help but wonder how she might one day ease those burdens. Maybe the scrap shop idea would help. Maybe there was something else ; some way to harness the quiet whispers she sensed in the Great Tree. But that thought felt too vague to pin down just yet.

She busied herself tidying the table and checking the pot of oil. It was still warm, but not dangerously so. The dough in the mixing bowl needed a bit more time to rise, so there wasn't much else to do. After a final pass around the yard ; shooing away a stray chicken that had wandered back ; she wiped her hands on her skirt and decided the time was right. She'd do as she promised: see Niya and Mandla, and maybe gather a few leads on broken items folks wanted fixed.

Naledi stepped away from the hut and made her way along the dusty path that snaked between the other little homes of the village. She nodded and smiled at neighbors who lounged outside, greeting them with a polite "Morning." Some responded in kind, others seemed too preoccupied to notice. Children not much younger than Naledi scurried around, chasing a tattered ball or squealing as they played tag among the goats. The warm air carried an undercurrent of hope ; market days always stirred a sense of possibility, no matter how modest the setting.

Just past the last hut, the Great Tree's massive crown appeared. The morning light filtered through its leaves, casting dappled shadows on the ground. Naledi's heart lifted at the sight ; she'd only parted from it a short while ago, but it was like seeing an old friend. And though she desperately wanted to pause and feel the tree's bark under her palm, the promise of meeting Niya and Mandla drove her on.

Sure enough, she found them just beyond the Great Tree's shadow. Niya was hunched over a small wire basket, rummaging through bits of metal ; spoons with bent handles, lids missing knobs. Mandla knelt beside a pair of tin cups, tapping a small hammer against the rim of one to straighten a dent. They looked up in unison when Naledi approached.

"Hey!" Niya exclaimed, flashing a broad grin that showed a chipped front tooth Naledi always found endearing. "I was wondering if you'd come. Thought you might be stuck at home all day."

Naledi shook her head. "Mama and Boikonyo went off to the market. I finished my chores, so here I am. How's the haul looking?"

Mandla sighed dramatically, lifting one of the tin cups to show her the ragged edges where the handle had broken off. "It's a lot of work," he said, "but if we can salvage even half of this stuff, we can probably sell it for a coin or two. We're learning as we go."

"And if we fix them nicely," Niya interjected, "folks will see it's cheaper to buy refurbished pots than brand-new ones from traders. Word will spread."

Naledi felt a bubble of excitement rise in her chest. This was exactly what she needed: a taste of possibility, the sense that she wasn't just daydreaming under a tree but contributing to something tangible. "I can ask around," she offered. "Mama told me some neighbors might have broken knives or cracked plates they were going to throw away. If we fix those, we'll get more variety in our shop."

"Brilliant," Niya chirped, rummaging for a note she'd scribbled on a scrap of paper. "We wrote down a few names already. Old Miss Maseko said she's got a kettle that leaks at the bottom. Mr. Thema might give us those old hinges from his storehouse door. I'm telling you, we're about to corner the scrap market!" She giggled, half-joking but entirely enthusiastic.

Mandla tapped his hammer lightly on the ground, as if to punctuate Niya's words. "We just need a better name than 'scrap shop.' Maybe something that sounds… fancier."

"How about *Mandla's Marvels*?" Niya teased.

He snorted. "Too self-centered. We need to include you and Naledi."

They bantered good-naturedly for a moment, throwing out ridiculous ideas ; *Niya's Notions and Repairs*, *Naledi's New Life for Old Stuff* ; until all three were laughing so hard that a passing goat paused to stare at them in mild disapproval.

Finally, Naledi wiped a tear of laughter from the corner of her eye. She caught her breath and said, "We can think about the name later. For now, let's just find enough items to mend so we can show folks what we can do."

Mandla grinned, nodding. "We'll start by finishing these cups and utensils. Then we'll see if we can track down that kettle from Miss Maseko. Afterwards, we'll ; "

But his words were cut short by the shrill ring of a bell from the direction of the village center. All three children turned, instantly curious. The bell typically meant some announcement ; either a warning about a wandering hyena (not common but not unheard of) or news of traveling merchants passing through. Naledi felt her heart skip. Traveling merchants often meant fresh faces, maybe even new stories or items from far-off towns. For Zanele, it could mean stiffer competition or new opportunities. And for Naledi, it was another reminder that there was a wider world beyond the huts and the Great Tree.

"Come on," Niya said, stuffing the wire basket under a small cloth to hide it. "Let's go see what the fuss is about."

Naledi exchanged a glance with Mandla. Excitement pricked at the back of her neck ; who knew what was unfolding near the market stall where Zanele and Boikonyo were set up? For a moment, she wondered if her chores were truly finished, but then she decided it was important to know what was happening in the village, for her mother's sake too.

And so they took off at a brisk pace, winding their way back through the dust-laden paths, past the Great Tree whose leaves sighed gently in the breeze, as if wishing them well on their little adventure. Naledi cast a quick, grateful glance upward, silently promising she'd return to share whatever news she gathered. Then she joined her friends, stepping into the unfolding day ; hopeful, curious, and ready for whatever the world had in store.

WINDS ACROSS THE ROOF

A single bell had never seemed so loud. Its clang rang out clear as a rooster's crow, echoing across the sun-baked huts and stirring up a swirl of dust in the village center. Naledi, Niya, and Mandla hurried along the winding path, hearts pounding with excitement. The midday sun was near its zenith now, baking the rooftops and setting the ground aglow in a shimmer of wavy heat. Yet the three children paid no mind to the sweat beading on their foreheads ; they were too curious about the commotion ahead.

They arrived at the market area just in time to see folks gathering around a pair of newcomers. A small wagon, rickety in places but painted in cheerful blues and reds, stood near Zanele's stall. One of the newcomers was an older woman dressed in a bright shawl; the other was a lanky man with a broad-brimmed hat and kind eyes. Both bore the easy smiles of traveling traders who'd seen a hundred villages and expected to see a hundred more.

"What's going on?" Niya whispered, craning her neck to spot a glimpse of the wagon's contents. Mandla, a full head taller than her, tried to peer over the small crowd forming a loose circle.

Naledi slipped between two onlookers ; an old auntie with a

walking stick and a teenage boy with a basket of herbs ; and reached the front. There, she saw Zanele standing by her snack table, hands on her hips but an expression of polite interest on her face. Boikonyo hovered behind her with his usual frown, though he seemed more curious than disapproving for once.

"All right, folks," the lanky man was saying, doffing his hat with a theatrical bow. "My name's Otieno, and this here is my sister, Hadzi. We're travelers from the north, bringing wares from all over ; tools, trinkets, cloth, and a few surprises. Came to see if your fine village might need a thing or two."

Hadzi, the older woman, stepped forward to tug a corner of the wagon's cover aside. Beneath it lay a jumble of items: clay pots stacked precariously, wooden carvings wrapped in cloth, metal rods clinking softly against each other. "We've also got a few charms that folks might fancy," she added in a raspy, cheerful voice. "Handmade, if you don't mind the lumps and bumps."

A wave of soft chatter spread through the villagers. Some looked on with skepticism, others with the open-faced fascination that new things often bring to a place so remote. Naledi was somewhere in between ; half of her wanted to see every single item in that wagon, the other half was rooted to the spot, studying the travelers' expressions to decide whether they were friend or foe.

Zanele cleared her throat. "I see you found our market," she said, her voice kind but firm. "We don't get many wagons coming through. Where'd you say you were from?"

"From the north," Otieno repeated, glancing around the crowd. "We've been on the road for months now. Heard tell there's a string of villages out this way that don't see many traders. Figured we might do a good turn, if folks need supplies."

His sister, Hadzi, pointed to a battered chest in the back of the wagon. "We've got a few cloth rolls that might interest you," she said to Zanele, noticing her apron and quickly guessing she was the sort to fix clothes or patch things up. "Colors from faraway places ; blues, yellows, reds that'd make your eyes pop. We trade in coins or sometimes food. Whatever suits you."

Behind Zanele, Boikonyo grunted. "We're short on coins as is," he muttered, half to himself. "And we've got a roof to fix."

Zanele gave him a quick sidelong glance. "True," she said quietly, then raised her voice to address Otieno and Hadzi again. "What about tools? Nails, hammers, that sort of thing. My boy's right ; our roof needs mending."

Otieno's face brightened, as if he'd just remembered a pocketful of jewels. "Ah, nails! Indeed, I have some. Not a huge stock, mind, but enough to patch a roof, I reckon." He rummaged in a side compartment of the wagon and produced a small, well-worn box. Opening it, he revealed neat rows of iron nails, some short, some long. "These are from a forge near the big river. Solid quality."

Zanele's eyes lit up. Boikonyo leaned in, his usual scowl melting a bit at the sight of a potential solution to their roof woes. Naledi could almost see the relief flicker across his features ; maybe, just maybe, they'd have a proper fix before the rains came.

But Hadzi wasn't done. She glanced across the small audience, her eyes alighting on Naledi, Niya, and Mandla near the front. A teasing smile stretched over her lips. "We also got some things for the young ones. Toys, small instruments… if you're the kind that likes a bit of music."

Naledi's heart skipped. She nudged Niya, who perked up with interest. Mandla took a half-step forward, quietly curious. The wagon's cover was whipped further aside, revealing a painted chest. Hadzi reached for its latch.

"Toys and instruments?" Naledi breathed, half in disbelief. She couldn't recall the last time she'd seen anything more musical than a homemade drum or the occasional tin whistle at the market. Her father had been rumored to hum tunes sometimes ; though she barely remembered that, if it was even her own memory or just stories from others. The idea of an instrument from beyond the village set a swirl of excitement in her stomach.

"Oh yes," Hadzi said, lifting the chest's lid. Inside were small wooden figures, carved animals, and a half-dozen simple flutes carved out of bamboo. A rattle or two with beaded ends. She lifted one of the flutes delicately, turning it so the light caught the carved patterns. "We pick these up from different villages along the way," she explained. "Children love 'em. Sometimes grown-ups too, if they got music in their soul."

Zanele, busy examining nails with Boikonyo, caught Naledi's longing expression from the corner of her eye. "Careful, child," she warned gently. "We can't buy everything, you know."

"I know, Mama," Naledi managed to say, unable to tear her gaze from the flute. It had a soft gleam, the bamboo polished to a smooth finish. If she had a coin, maybe she could ; no, that was silly. Better to put the money toward nails for the roof. Still, her heart yearned in a way she hadn't felt before, and she wondered if the flute might sound like a bird singing at dawn, or if she'd even know how to hold it properly.

"Think we can trade something for one of these?" Niya whispered, stepping closer to the chest. Her eyes glowed at the array of little wonders inside: marbles made of colored glass, a child-sized drum with a taut hide stretched across the top. "Maybe we can fix something for them in exchange?"

Before Naledi could answer, Mandla leaned in, quietly rummaging through the pockets of his patched trousers. "I've got a few coins from the scrap shop idea," he whispered. "Not much, but maybe enough for one small thing."

Hadzi noticed their hushed conversation and beckoned them nearer with a friendly wave. "Come, take a closer look, young ones. If there's something that calls out to you, we'll see if we can't find a fair trade."

Niya, braver than both Naledi and Mandla, pointed to the half-dozen bamboo flutes. "How much are these?" she asked.

Hadzi pursed her lips, weighing the question. "That depends. Which one are you looking at? Some are simpler, some have fancier carvings. We like to trade or sell them for a coin or two ; maybe three for the really nice ones. Or something else if it's a good bargain."

Mandla fiddled with the coins in his hand, biting his lip. Naledi's heart fluttered. She couldn't possibly ask him to spend his coins on her. Yet she couldn't deny the flute was enchanting. She reached out tentatively, fingers hovering just above the carved bamboo.

But just then, a new voice cut through the midday air: "Now what's all this crowd about?"

Naledi turned to see Mama Lindiwe, the elderly neighbor who'd once told her that old trees carry memories. Clutching her walking stick, Mama Lindiwe ambled forward, scanning the wagon's contents with a shrewd eye. "Travelers, hmm?"

"Yes, ma'am," Otieno replied, tipping his hat as politely as he had for everyone else. "Looking to do fair trade."

Mama Lindiwe's gaze settled on the children and the small chest of toys and instruments, but then she flashed a half-toothless grin. "Ah, you youngsters always got your eyes on something shiny," she said, chuckling. She leaned closer to Naledi and patted her arm. "Let me guess: you're wanting that flute, child?"

Naledi blushed. "It's pretty," she admitted, feeling as though Mama Lindiwe had read her thoughts.

Mama Lindiwe nodded. "Nothing wrong with music. We had more of it in the old days, you know ; drums, singing, dancing under the moon." She sighed, her voice trailing off with nostalgia. "Maybe we could use a bit more music in these parts. Times are tough enough without it."

Niya took that as encouragement. "We can ask Malume Nathi, too," she suggested in a hushed tone. "He might have something to trade, or maybe he wants to buy something from Otieno and Hadzi. Then we can fix it and resell ; like a chain deal."

Mandla perked up at the idea. "Hey, that's not bad. The more business we do, the more we can invest in stuff we actually want."

Naledi listened to their chatter, part of her alight with possibility, another part still feeling the weight of responsibility. Across the way, Boikonyo was in earnest talk with Otieno about the price of nails, while Zanele stood beside him, carefully counting coins in her hand. Naledi knew the roof had to come first. She'd seen the way the sun sometimes slanted through the weak spots, revealing dusty beams that could collapse if pounded by hard rain. She couldn't possibly ask Mama to spare money for a flute.

As if reading her mind, Mama Lindiwe nudged her gently. "You got that hungry look in your eyes, child. Sometimes life doesn't wait for the perfect time. Sometimes you find a tune that needs playing right when everything else feels broken. Don't dismiss your heart's longing so quick."

Naledi felt tears prick her eyes. She swallowed. "Maybe I can earn it," she said, almost to herself. "If we fix enough broken scraps, or help around the market, maybe I can save up."

Mama Lindiwe's grin widened. "Now that's the spirit."

Just then, Otieno finished speaking with Boikonyo and turned back to the little group. "All settled on them nails," he said. "Your mother and brother are good at bargaining, I'll give 'em that." He patted the wagon's side and looked at the children. "So, how 'bout you youngsters? Anything you want to trade or buy? I hear there might be a small scrap shop in the works?"

Niya chuckled, not at all fazed by the fact that rumors traveled fast around a tiny village. "We don't have much right now," she admitted, "but maybe we can talk about it. We fix broken pots, cups, stuff like that. If you've got items nobody else wants, we might be able to repair and resell them."

Mandla nodded eagerly. "We've got some skill, and we're learning more every day."

Hadzi gave them a slow nod of interest. "Might be I have a few battered spoons or a dented kettle. We usually toss 'em or trade 'em for scraps. If you can fix them and make a profit, good on you."

A hush fell for a moment, and Naledi felt at the brink of something exciting. A bigger web of trade ; first the old spoons, then fix them up, sell them to neighbors, earn a coin or two. Perhaps enough for a flute. She glanced at Zanele, who was tucking a small box of nails into her basket. Her mother caught her eye and offered a soft nod, as if to say, *Yes, child, I see your hopes. Go on.*

"Let's see what you've got," Mandla said, trying to sound confident despite being a mere boy in a village not used to big deals. Niya wore a grin from ear to ear, the idea of more business lighting her spirit.

Hadzi rummaged in the wagon's far corner, pulling out a small burlap sack. "Here," she said, placing it on the ground and untieing the top. Inside were a few dented metal utensils ; forks missing tines, spoons with twisted handles ; and a short kettle with a battered rim. "Nothing fancy, but if you've the know-how, you can salvage them."

Niya crouched down, picking up a spoon. "We'll fix the shape, maybe polish the metal. For the kettle, we can hammer out the dent and reattach the handle. Might be worth something at the market."

Hadzi raised a bushy eyebrow. "You talk like you know your stuff. All right, I'll trade you these for… oh, a few helpings of your best snacks, plus maybe a small coin if you can spare it. I got a weakness for sweet fritters."

Niya and Mandla exchanged a look, then glanced at Naledi. She had just enough sense to speak up: "My mother sells fritters, and I bet we can get you some. We might have a coin from our scrap business we started. Not a lot, but enough for a partial trade."

"Deal," Hadzi said, extending her hand in a flourish of finality.

While Niya and Mandla began to haggle the details, Naledi found her gaze drifting back to the chest of instruments. One flute in particular, carved with a delicate swirl pattern, seemed to call out to her. She dared to lift it from the chest, feeling the smooth bamboo against her palm. For a moment, she imagined bringing it to her lips, maybe coaxing out a soft melody that could float on the evening breeze beneath the Great Tree. A wave of longing rolled through her, as sweet and haunting as any tune she could dream up.

She swallowed. *Not yet,* she told herself. *Maybe soon.*

Slipping the flute gently back into the chest, she resolved to work twice as hard with Niya and Mandla, to fix up every broken kettle, pot, and spoon they could get their hands on. If she could earn her own coin ; truly earn it ; then maybe, just maybe, she could return to Otieno and Hadzi. Maybe she could trade for that flute and bring a new music to the village, a sound that might echo under the Great Tree's branches and remind them all that, even when times were tough, a melody could still rise above it all.

As the midday sun blazed overhead, the crowd around the wagon began to disperse, each villager returning to chores or pausing for a meal. Zanele, her basket of nails tucked safely at her side, headed back toward the hut with Boikonyo, who was already talking about how quickly they could patch up the roof. Niya and Mandla, brimming with excitement over their new acquisitions, packed the battered utensils into a small crate they'd borrowed. And Naledi lingered just a moment longer, offering a grateful smile to Otieno and Hadzi.

"Thank you," she said softly, though it covered more than just the scraps they'd traded. It covered the possibility of that flute, still resting in the wagon's chest, waiting for someone to give it life.

The siblings both bowed in unison, as if Naledi were a dignitary. "We'll be around for a few days," Otieno said. "If you change your mind, you know where to find us."

She nodded, heart thumping with a strange mix of hope and uncertainty. The day was not yet over, and already it seemed to pulse with opportunity. For a brief second, her thoughts flickered to the Great Tree ; would it approve of these strangers, these new trades, these new dreams?

She turned, rejoining Niya and Mandla as they hurried off to plan their scrap repairs. In the distance, a handful of crows alighted on the Great Tree's highest branches, cawing into the golden sky. Though Naledi couldn't be sure, she almost imagined the leaves rustled in reply ; a soft, leafy applause for the promise of something new in the village, something that might just lead Naledi toward her own hidden song.

WHISPERING ROOTS

A mid-afternoon sun cast tall shadows across the village, giving everything a dappled, golden sheen ; like someone had draped a warm glow over the huts and yard. Naledi stood under the Great Tree, shifting from one foot to the other, her mind swirling with all that had happened earlier in the day. New travelers, potential tools for fixing the roof, dented utensils to mend for the scrap shop ; and that flute, shining in the wagon like a beckoning promise.

She inhaled deeply, letting the tree's shade envelop her. "You saw all that, didn't you?" she murmured, fingertips brushing the tree's rough bark. A gentle breeze rattled the leaves overhead, as though the old giant was kindly humoring her. Naledi knew it was just the wind, but in her heart of hearts, she liked to believe the tree listened.

Her thoughts broke when she heard approaching footsteps and cheerful voices. Rounding the corner of the widest root, Niya appeared, the wire basket from earlier perched on her hip. Mandla trailed behind, lugging a small crate full of battered spoons and forks. Both wore satisfied grins, like they'd just unearthed a treasure trove.

"Hey, Naledi!" Niya called, waving. "We've been looking for you. Did you slip away from your chores?"

Naledi smiled, half-guilty. "Mama's busy counting up the day's sales, and Boikonyo's sorting those nails for the roof. I finished cleaning up, so... here I am."

Mandla hefted the crate onto a low root, letting out a sigh of relief. "We've got a serious haul. Hadzi gave us two more spoons and a kettle because she liked Zanele's fritters so much. Guess sweet treats make for easy bartering."

Niya giggled, rummaging in her wire basket. "We figure if we can fix these pieces by tomorrow's market, we can sell them. Then maybe we'll have enough coin to expand our business." She shot Naledi a sly look. "Or spend it on something we really want."

Naledi knew exactly what Niya hinted at. Her cheeks warmed. She'd told them both about the bamboo flute and how it made her heart leap in her chest. "I'm not sure about that," she said softly. "The roof still needs fixing. And Mama... well, she wants every coin accounted for."

Mandla rested his hand on the rim of the crate. "Sure, but not every coin has to go to the roof, right? If we make a profit from these repairs, it's our money to keep. We can split it three ways."

Niya nodded vigorously. "You could use your share to buy the flute, or at least put it on hold. Maybe the travelers would let you pay bit by bit."

Naledi swallowed, trying not to let hope flutter too wildly in her chest. "It feels selfish, though. I mean, the roof ; "

"Is your mother's concern," Mandla interjected gently, "and your brother's. We're not stealing from them. We're just using our own skills to earn something. That's fair and square."

Niya rubbed Naledi's shoulder. "Besides, you've done plenty to help around your home. Don't you deserve something that's just for you?"

A hush fell among them. The Great Tree's leaves rustled again, sending dappled sunlight dancing across their faces. Naledi could almost imagine the tree encouraging her to take a step toward this dream. She sighed. "All right, let's see how much we earn first. If we fix everything by tomorrow, maybe we'll have an idea of the profit."

"Deal," Mandla said, clapping his hands. "Let's get to work, then."

They settled on a flat patch of earth right under the tree's canopy, laying out the kettle and spoons. Mandla knelt beside the crate, producing a small hammer and an improvised anvil ; a chunk of scrap metal Malume Nathi had given him. Niya took out a rag and a small jar of polish they'd managed to mix from ash, water, and a pinch of leftover oil. Naledi set about wiping off the worst of the rust and grime.

As Mandla hammered a particularly stubborn dent in the kettle, Naledi glanced up. "What do we charge once these are fixed?" she asked.

Niya shrugged. "Depends on how they look. If we can make them nearly new, maybe a few coins each. If they still look rough, we might price them lower."

"This one's shaping up well," Mandla grunted, tapping the kettle with measured force. "If I can straighten the handle and seal that leak, someone might buy it for a decent price."

Naledi couldn't hide her excitement. "You're good at this," she said, admiration coloring her voice. "Where'd you learn to hammer metal like that?"

Mandla paused, swiping sweat from his brow. "My uncle used to fix pots and farm tools. I watched him now and then. Never thought I'd do it myself, but here we are."

Niya beamed. "I'm just good at numbers, but Mandla's the real craftsman. And you, Naledi" ; she raised an eyebrow ; "you're the one who talks to people. You'll be the face of our enterprise."

Naledi blushed. "All I do is smile and say hello."

"That's more than most folks," Niya teased, returning to her polishing. "Besides, you've got a sweet, friendly way about you. People trust you." She paused. "And speaking of trust... you think your mother will trust us enough to let you come out to the market tomorrow with these?"

"I hope so," Naledi replied. "Mama's usually busy at her own stall, so maybe she'll be glad I'm doing something useful. Boikonyo might grumble, but he's always grumbling."

They laughed at the image of Boikonyo's perpetual scowl. Though Naledi felt a twinge of guilt ; her brother worked so hard, and he worried about so much. *Maybe one day,* she thought, *he'll see that my daydreams aren't a waste.*

They spent the better part of an hour methodically restoring each spoon and the kettle. Mandla hammered out dents, Niya polished and tested for leaks, and Naledi used a small cloth to wipe away any remaining grime. Now and then, passersby drifted past the tree, throwing them curious smiles or offering pointers. An older woman, carrying a basket on her head, paused to say, "You three look mighty determined. Good luck, my little fixers!" Then she went on her way, humming a tune that echoed strangely off the thick trunk.

At last, they set their tools aside, leaning back to admire their handiwork. The spoons looked almost new ; shiny enough to catch the reflection of the leaves overhead. The kettle boasted a sturdy handle and a near-invisible patch where the hole had been. Even Niya seemed impressed, holding it up so sunlight glinted off the metal surface.

"That's a job well done," she declared, nodding firmly. "Let's see if we can sell these tomorrow."

Mandla wiped a spot of grease from his cheek, flashing a triumphant grin. "I'm in. Might help if we make a sign or something, so people know we're selling scraps."

Naledi giggled. "People will know, trust me. Word spreads fast here."

They tidied up their tools and slipped the spoons and kettle into Niya's wire basket. Shadows were lengthening across the ground now ; afternoon leaning toward evening. Naledi guessed Zanele would be starting supper soon, if she'd finished counting the day's coins.

"Come on," Mandla said, picking up his hammer and scrap-metal anvil. "Let's walk Naledi home. We can drop by Miss Maseko's place on the way, see if she's got those broken hinges she talked about."

Niya adjusted the basket on her hip. "That's the plan. And Naledi, if we get enough items, we'll have a full stall one day. Then maybe you can stand there playing your flute ; once you get it ; and we'll draw a crowd!"

Naledi's heart fluttered at the thought, yet she kept her excitement in check. "One step at a time," she murmured with a smile.

They started down the path, chatter filling the air with easy camaraderie. Naledi felt a contentment she could hardly describe ; like the future was bright, stretching out beneath the Great Tree's wide branches. Sure, there were chores to do and a roof to fix, but there was also laughter, enterprise, and a secret wish for something more.

The trio passed a couple of villagers on their way ; an older man tipping his hat in greeting, a group of children playing a clapping game near a goat pen. Finally, they reached Miss Maseko's hut, which leaned slightly more than most, the remnants of an old paint job peeling from the walls. A mangy cat lounged by the doorway, tail flicking in lazy disinterest.

Miss Maseko herself emerged at the sound of their approach ; a wiry woman with sharp eyes and an even sharper tongue when it suited her. "What do you three want?" she asked, hands on her hips.

Niya took the lead, her voice bright with confidence. "Afternoon, Miss Maseko! We heard you might have some broken hinges to get rid of. We're fixing metal scraps these days."

The older woman raised an eyebrow. "Oh, you are, are you? Well, good luck. Those hinges are more rust than metal at this point. I was about to toss 'em."

"We can try to repair them," Mandla said, stepping forward. "If they're beyond saving, we'll just scrap 'em completely. But if they can be fixed, we'll pay you a fair price ; or cut you a deal if you need something else mended."

Miss Maseko snorted softly, though not unkindly. "You three got spunk, I'll give you that. Wait here." She disappeared into her hut, the cat eyeing them suspiciously before slinking off.

Naledi exchanged a smile with Niya. She couldn't help but admire how Niya handled herself ; straightforward but polite, never letting doubt seep into her tone. Mandla, too, had a sturdy calm about him, as if nothing phased him quite as much as a tough dent or two. Naledi felt a fresh surge of gratitude to be part of their little team.

When Miss Maseko returned, she carried two hinges that had clearly seen better days. They were caked in rust, one side bent almost beyond recognition. She held them out, a skeptic's glint in her eye. "Here. Do your worst."

Mandla took them gently, frowning at the state of the metal. "Yeah, these are pretty far gone," he muttered, but there was a layer of excitement under his concern ; like an artist challenged by a particularly tricky canvas.

Miss Maseko waved a dismissive hand. "You fix 'em, you can keep 'em or sell 'em, makes no difference to me. But if you manage to get 'em working, come let me know. I might need a hinge or two for that rickety chicken coop of mine." A grudging smile twitched at her lips. "I'll pay a coin or some eggs, whichever suits."

Mandla grinned. "Thank you, Miss Maseko. We'll do our best."

With that, they said their goodbyes, tucking the hinges into Niya's basket with the rest of their items. As they headed down the path toward Naledi's hut, the sun had begun dipping behind distant hills, painting the sky in purples and oranges. The warm light caressed the village, turning every roof and wall into a silhouette against a fiery backdrop.

Reaching Naledi's yard, they spotted Zanele near the doorway, shaking out a cloth. Boikonyo was just inside, arms folded, watching the evening sky with a pensive expression. The sight of them reminded Naledi that day's end would bring chores, supper, and discussions about tomorrow's tasks ; but somehow she didn't mind. She felt more purposeful than ever, with Niya and Mandla at her side.

"Hey, Mama," Naledi called, trotting ahead. "We found some more scraps to fix ; this time from Miss Maseko!"

Zanele turned, smiling at Niya and Mandla. "Well, you three are keeping busy, aren't you? Good on you. Boikonyo's been talking about nails all afternoon, so it's a house full of repairs here."

Niya chuckled. "We'll leave you to it, then. Naledi, meet us tomorrow morning by the tree if you can, okay? We'll see if we can get these hinges hammered into something useful."

"Sounds like a plan," Naledi agreed, cheeks warm with anticipation. "Thanks, both of you."

After Niya and Mandla departed, Zanele gestured for Naledi to join her by the door. "Long day, hmm?"

Naledi nodded. "We did a lot, Mama. Mandla fixed a kettle, Niya polished spoons, and ; well, we might sell them in the morning.

We're calling it a 'scrap shop,' sort of."

Zanele placed a gentle hand on Naledi's shoulder. "I'm proud of you," she said softly. "You're finding your own ways to help, and that matters."

A wave of relief washed over Naledi. "Thank you, Mama," she whispered. A small part of her longed to tell her mother all about the bamboo flute, to confess how badly she wanted it. But she decided to wait ; better to show she could earn it first.

Together, they entered the hut, where Boikonyo offered a curt nod before setting aside the nails he'd been counting. Supper consisted of leftover fritters and a simple stew Zanele had managed to whip up, and the warmth of the meal settled in Naledi's stomach like a gentle reassurance. She stole a glance at Boikonyo, noticing how the tension across his brow softened once or twice when talk turned to the roof repairs.

Later, after the dishes were cleaned and the yard was quiet, Naledi stepped outside to gaze at the Great Tree under the glow of a half-moon. She let the evening breeze brush against her cheeks, the tree's branches swaying like a lullaby. She thought of the battered kettle, now looking almost brand new, and of the hinges Miss Maseko said were beyond saving ; but might yet serve a purpose. A pang of longing surfaced for the flute, which remained in Otieno and Hadzi's wagon. She wondered if, in the hush of night, it might be singing its own silent tune.

Just like these scraps, she told herself, *something broken can be mended and made beautiful again.* Maybe that was true of more than just pots and spoons. Maybe it was true of roofs, families ; dreams. For the first time, she felt a swell of certainty that her daydreams weren't idle ; they were seeds, waiting for a chance to root and grow.

She rested a hand on the Great Tree's trunk, wishing it goodnight, letting the bark's ancient texture ground her thoughts. Then she turned for the hut, heart full of both hope and the sweet hum of something more ; something like the music she hoped one day to play, perhaps right here under these broad, watchful branches.

SEEDS OF FRIENDSHIP, BRANCHES OF HOPE

Dawn crept into the village with a gentle hush, the sun peeking shyly over the hills as though it, too, wanted to see if the day's plans might pan out. Naledi stirred awake to the sound of muffled voices ; Zanele and Boikonyo in low conversation at the front of the hut. She stretched, rubbed her eyes, and glanced at the little window. A thin band of soft light fell across the floorboards, promising a bright morning if the clouds held off.

The hut felt unusually calm. Usually, by the time Naledi opened her eyes, Zanele would already be fussing about breakfast or preparing dough for her snacks, while Boikonyo stomped around making a racket about chores. Today, though, a sort of quiet cooperation seemed to settle over the place. Perhaps the new nails had lifted Boikonyo's spirits ; he had a plan for that roof now, and a plan always steadied him. Naledi smiled to herself, rising from her thin mat and slipping on her sandals with care.

She stepped outside to find Zanele, arms folded, surveying the early sky. She wore a simple headscarf and that calm, determined expression that often graced her features when she was trying to mentally organize the day. Boikonyo was off near the corner of the hut, studying a piece of broken wood siding that had seen better days.

"Mama," Naledi said softly, rubbing the last of the sleep from her eyes, "I'm heading to school soon. Need me to do anything first?"

Zanele turned at the sound of her daughter's voice, her lips curving into a half-smile. "Morning, child. If you could fetch a small jug of water for the leftover dough, that'd be a help. I'll fry up another batch of fritters once you're gone."

Naledi nodded, grabbing the clay jug that stood by the door. Even though the morning air was cool, she could already sense the promise of heat later ; this was a land that rarely stayed mild for long. She glanced at Boikonyo, who was testing the rotten wood with a push of his palm, and gave him a polite "Good morning."

He grunted an acknowledgment. "I'll be hauling up the roof thatch soon," he said, not taking his eyes from the siding. "If you see Mandla, tell him I might need help. Kid knows how to swing a hammer."

Naledi's eyebrows rose in surprise ; Boikonyo rarely praised Mandla. "Sure," she said, then hurried off with the jug, her sandals scuffing the dust.

The communal well, as ever, was a small hive of early-morning bustle. A few neighbors were already waiting, trading yawns and gossip while they lowered buckets for the day's water. Naledi found her place in line, let her thoughts drift momentarily to the new items she and her friends had fixed, and how she might show them off soon enough.

"I saw your mother's fritters were a hit again," one older neighbor remarked, tapping a foot impatiently while the bucket was lowered for the next person. "Travelers said they were the best in the region."

Naledi smiled politely. "Mama's got a knack," she agreed. "It's how we manage."

Once she'd filled her jug, she hurried back home, passing it off to Zanele. A faint smell of frying dough wafted from inside the hut already, making Naledi's stomach grumble. She longed to linger for a bite, but she was mindful that school started soon, and Niya and Mandla would be waiting.

"I'm off," she told Zanele, giving her mother a quick hug. Zanele patted her head in return, her hands still dusted with flour.

"Stay focused in class," Zanele said, her voice firm but kind. "And if you see Niya, give her my thanks for those sweet polish rags she shared the other day."

Naledi promised she would. Slinging her small cloth bag over her shoulder, she set off toward the modest schoolhouse on the village's far side.

Unlike the bustling markets or the hush beneath the Great Tree, the schoolyard possessed an air of ordered liveliness. A row of children, some younger and some older than Naledi, had formed a ragtag line by the single door. Others sat on the wide porch, waiting for the teacher ; a stern but fair woman named Ms. Dlamini ; to call them in.

Naledi spotted Niya almost immediately, leaning against one of the schoolhouse posts. She wore a big grin, her braided hair tied back with a piece of cloth. Mandla, taller by a good head, stood next to her, fiddling with a little tin whistle he'd found in the scraps. His attempts at blowing through it produced a faint, squeaky note that caused a few of the littler kids to giggle.

"There you are," Niya exclaimed, beckoning Naledi over. "We were just about to go in. The teacher's late, as usual, so we've got a minute."

Mandla saluted Naledi with the tin whistle. "Morning. Heard

Boikonyo might need help with the roof. Guess I'd better keep my schedule open for that."

Naledi smirked. "He actually asked about you. Must be a miracle."

Niya let out a hearty laugh. "Or he finally noticed how good Mandla is with tools." She gently nudged Mandla's arm. "Show Naledi what else you brought."

Mandla grinned, setting the whistle aside and digging into his satchel. Out came a small, polished spoon ; one of the scraps they'd repaired to near perfection the day before. The metal gleamed in the morning sun, a testament to their teamwork. "We're going to show Ms. Dlamini later, see if she might want to buy one for the school's lunch set. Or at least let us display it somewhere for folks to see."

Naledi's eyes lit up. "That's beautiful. Hard to believe it was all bent and rusty."

"Just needed some TLC," Niya teased, adjusting a loose braid. "Anyway, we've got class first. Then we can talk to her after. You still good to help us advertise these at the next market day?"

"Absolutely," Naledi said, feeling a small swirl of excitement in her stomach. "If I'm not busy with Mama's stall, I'll definitely come."

Before they could discuss further, a call rang out across the yard. "All right, children, line up for class!" Ms. Dlamini stood at the doorway, her hands perched on her hips. She was a tall woman in a neat but simple dress, her hair tied in a tight bun. "Let's move ; no dilly-dallying!"

The group shuffled into a semblance of a line, with Niya, Naledi, and Mandla at the rear. Inside the schoolhouse, the walls were adorned with makeshift charts and a chalkboard, where Ms. Dlamini usually wrote out lessons in neat script. Wooden desks, some wobbly from years of use, filled the room in two rows.

A small window near the front let in precious light, which flickered across dust motes dancing in the air.

"Settle down," Ms. Dlamini commanded, tapping her chalk against the board. "We'll start with a little arithmetic this morning."

A few groans sounded, but Naledi and Niya exchanged grins ; Niya loved numbers, and Naledi felt a secret thrill at the idea that she'd become handier with math lately, counting coins for her mother's snack stall. Mandla was less enthusiastic, but he still slid into his seat without complaint, eyes occasionally drifting to the tin whistle on the corner of his desk.

The lesson began with simple addition and multiplication, Ms. Dlamini calling on students at random to solve problems on the board. Niya hopped up eagerly when chosen, effortlessly rattling off correct sums. Naledi followed suit a moment later, her own calculations careful but right all the same. Mandla managed a passable attempt, though he blushed when Ms. Dlamini corrected his multiplication of larger numbers. Still, no one teased him; in a village school as small as this, everyone understood each other's strengths and weaknesses.

As the day wore on, the class covered reading, a bit of local geography, and even some basic science about crops and irrigation ; a vital topic for a community that relied on the land for survival. Naledi listened intently, her mind wandering occasionally to thoughts of the Great Tree and the battered items they'd fixed. She wondered what new wonders or travelers might come through the village next, maybe bringing instruments or more scraps. *Stop daydreaming,* she told herself, but a tiny spark of curiosity refused to dim.

When the midday break arrived, Ms. Dlamini gave them leave to stretch their legs and eat whatever lunch they had. Most children spilled out into the sunlit yard, racing to claim shady spots under the school's patchy awning. Niya, Mandla, and

Naledi gathered by an old tree stump near the side of the schoolhouse, taking out their meager lunches ; small rolls, leftover maize cakes, or a piece of fruit.

Niya devoured a handful of roasted peanuts, licking the salt from her fingers as she mulled over a new scheme. "So," she began, turning to Naledi and Mandla, "I was thinking: if Ms. Dlamini doesn't buy the spoon, maybe we can go around to the bigger huts in the village ; like Mr. Thema's storehouse ; see if they need cutlery or fixed items. We can do it after school, or tomorrow if we're free."

Mandla nodded, chewing on a piece of fruit. "Yeah, plus your brother needs me for the roof, but that might not take all day. If we can squeeze in a few stops, we'll gather orders for more scrap repairs. Then we can mention the kettle and the spoons. Maybe even the battered hinges from Miss Maseko, if I can straighten them out."

Naledi's eyes flickered with excitement. "We should also talk to Malume Nathi ; he might have some small items that need fixing. He always seems to have a pile of metal odds and ends lying around his shop."

Niya clapped her hands softly. "Exactly! And Naledi, you're our best spokesperson. People like you ; you're polite and patient. Me, I sometimes just blurt out the cost. Mandla is good at fixing, but he's not so much for the sales talk."

Mandla laughed, flicking a peanut shell at Niya's foot. "We each have our roles, right? So let's do it. After class, we approach Ms. Dlamini about the spoon. If that fails, we head around the village tomorrow."

With the plan set, they finished their small lunches and ambled around, enjoying a slight breeze that occasionally passed through. Schoolmates were scattered about, some playing a clapping game, others practicing multiplication on a scrap of slate. Two younger kids sat quietly, heads bent together, whispering about a rumored traveling show that might pass through. Naledi's ears perked at the mention of a show ; could it be Otieno and Hadzi had something more than just wares to sell? She stored the thought away for later.

When Ms. Dlamini called them back in, the trio took their seats, steeling themselves for another round of reading and writing. Naledi did her best to pay attention, but her mind kept drifting to the battered kettle, the freshly polished spoons, and the sparkle of possibility glinting on every piece of repaired metal. She forced herself to concentrate, scribbling letters in her exercise book, determined not to let daydreams derail her from the basics.

An hour later, Ms. Dlamini gave the class a quick break to tidy up and wash the blackboard. As Niya and Mandla helped gather used chalk and erase the board, Naledi approached the teacher with the newly polished spoon in hand. It trembled slightly in her grasp ; her nerves always kicked in when speaking to adults in an official capacity.

"Ma'am," she said timidly, "we wanted to show you something."

Ms. Dlamini glanced up, adjusting her glasses. "Yes, Naledi?"

Naledi took a breath, then held out the spoon. "My friends and I… we've been fixing metal scraps. This was rusted and bent, but Mandla hammered it straight, Niya polished it, and I cleaned off the last bits of grime. We call it our… scrap shop project."

The teacher accepted the spoon, her expression curious. She turned it over, inspecting the smooth handle and the gleaming curve. "Remarkable," she said at length, glancing over at Niya and Mandla, who had joined them. "You did all this yourselves?"

Mandla cleared his throat, suddenly shy. "Yes, ma'am. We're trying to earn a bit of coin ; help our families, maybe buy some proper tools. And, well… Naledi mentioned you might need a new spoon here at school?"

Ms. Dlamini considered the polished metal again. "We do go through spoons and forks rather fast with the little ones sometimes bending them. Though the school's budget is small..." She sighed. "But you've done fine work. If I can manage a coin or two, I'll consider buying it ; provided you promise to keep your studies up."

Niya's face lit up like a lantern. "Oh, we will, Ms. Dlamini. We love school."

A small, indulgent smile crossed the teacher's lips. "All right, then. Let's see. I'll speak with the head teacher about purchasing a few items for the school's kitchen. If it's approved, we'll pay a fair price." She held out the spoon to Naledi. "Hold onto it for now, and remind me in a day or two."

Thrilled, Naledi nodded. "Thank you, Ma'am!" she said, scooping the spoon back into her hands.

Ms. Dlamini fixed them with a kind, if stern, look. "Remember ; focus on your lessons, too. Don't let these business ambitions distract you from the fundamentals."

"Yes, Ma'am," the three chimed in near-unison, hearts soaring as they retreated to their desks.

The final stretch of school passed in a blur, Naledi barely containing the buzz of excitement swirling in her chest. When Ms. Dlamini finally dismissed them for the day, the trio burst outside, the afternoon sun greeting them like an old friend.

"She might really buy it!" Niya exclaimed, practically hopping in place.

Mandla pumped a fist in the air. "And if the school buys one, maybe they'll buy more. We fix enough spoons, forks, maybe a kettle for storing water? That could be a steady income."

Naledi clutched the spoon, still marveling at how shiny it looked. "We can do this," she said, feeling a resolve firm in her belly. "But Mandla, you'd better go see Boikonyo if he needs help."

He patted his satchel where the tin whistle rested. "I'll go now. Meet you two later by the Great Tree if you want? After supper, maybe we can plan tomorrow's errands."

They agreed, parting ways with bright waves. Niya took off toward her own home, while Naledi headed for the dusty path that would lead her back to Zanele's hut. Her stride felt lighter than usual, each step brimming with confidence. She pictured the flute once more, hidden among Otieno and Hadzi's traveling wagon. *If we do well enough…* she mused, the words dancing through her mind in time with her footsteps.

As she neared her hut, the rhythmic thunk of a hammer told her Boikonyo was already working. Sure enough, he stood by the side of the roof, strips of new thatch at his feet, a row of nails perched on a small ledge. Mandla's voice drifted from somewhere above; he must've climbed the ladder to help secure the patch. Through the open doorway, Naledi spotted Zanele kneading dough. But for once, the hush around the yard felt optimistic, like everyone was pulling in the same direction.

"Hey there, child," Zanele called from inside, noticing Naledi's return. "How was school?"

Naledi opened her mouth, ready to share all the news about Ms. Dlamini and the spoon. But first, she set it on the small table by the door, carefully untying her bag so it wouldn't jostle. "Mama," she said, stepping in, "it was good. I have a story to tell you ; about a teacher who might just buy one of the spoons we fixed."

Zanele's brows rose. "Oh? Well, don't keep me waiting."

Naledi glanced at the door frame, listening to the steady hammering outside, the comforting swirl of flour inside, and the memory of Ms. Dlamini's nod of approval. A sense of hope filled her chest ; hope that she could balance both work and wonder, that a bit of enterprise might lead to brighter tomorrows.

She took a deep breath. "So, there's this 'scrap shop' we've got going on..."

And as she recounted the day's events ; the triumphant display of the repaired spoon, Ms. Dlamini's possible interest, and Niya's idea to approach more neighbors ; she could swear the faintest rustle outside was the Great Tree, listening as well. Because some part of her believed that even a tree grown old with time could delight in the small victories of a girl who was beginning to find her place in a wide, dusty world.

TREASURES IN THE DUST

When the morning lessons ended on the day after Ms. Dlamini first admired that polished spoon, Naledi found her feet bouncing with anticipation. She'd passed every class exercise with near-flying colors, even scribbling her answers in record time, but her heart wasn't fully in the arithmetic or grammar. Instead, her mind kept drifting to the "scrap shop," the kettle and spoons they'd repaired, and the roof back at her family's hut ; which, by now, might be patched enough to keep any stray rains out. Whenever she thought of home, an ember of warmth kindled inside her. She was itching to see whether Boikonyo and Mandla had made progress, and even more so, she longed to check in with Niya about the rest of their scrap inventory.

As soon as Ms. Dlamini dismissed them for the day, Naledi hurried to the schoolyard's edge where Niya was waiting ; leaning casually against a low fence. Mandla, balancing his tin whistle between thumb and forefinger, stood nearby, testing out a few squeaky notes that made a gaggle of younger students giggle.

"You ready?" Niya asked with a grin. "I've been thinking all morning about how we can pitch our scrap fixes to Mr. Thema and some of the bigger families."

"More than ready," Naledi replied, adjusting the cloth bag slung over her shoulder. "Mama was up early frying dough again, so I didn't get to talk with her about the next market day. But I think she'll be supportive. You know how she is ; just happy I'm staying busy in a good way."

Mandla slipped the whistle into his satchel with a wry smile. "I swear I'll get a tune out of this thing yet, but not until it stops squeaking like a barn mouse." He pointed the whistle at Naledi. "You want to head home, or come with us to find Miss Maseko? She might have more scrap."

Naledi's face lit up, but she shook her head. "I should check on Boikonyo first. He and you were patching the roof, right? Did you finish?"

"Almost," Mandla said. "I left him hammering away before school started this morning. He told me not to skip class, so I hustled here. I'll probably help him more this afternoon if he hasn't killed his thumbs by then."

Niya snorted. "See if he's in a decent mood. If yes, we might rope him into telling the neighbors how good our repairs are." She shrugged. "He's got a way of, well… commanding attention."

Naledi suppressed a giggle. "Commanding's one word for it," she teased. "All right, how about this: I'll drop by home, see about the roof and my chores, then meet you both under the Great Tree in about an hour? We can decide which houses to visit for new scrap."

"Perfect," Niya and Mandla chimed together. They parted ways, with Niya and Mandla strolling off toward Miss Maseko's place, while Naledi trotted in the opposite direction, the dusty path crunching underfoot.

The sun was sliding toward its midday peak, making the heat

shimmer like invisible waves across the village lanes. Naledi kept her pace steady but brisk, greeting a few neighbors along the way. Here and there, she glimpsed signs of small improvements ; someone had hammered a fresh board over a broken window, another had rigged a makeshift fence from recycled scraps. It struck her that maybe the idea of fixing and reusing was catching on. That possibility brought a hopeful spring to her step.

When she reached her family's hut, the first thing she spotted was a newly secured patch of thatch on the roof. Boikonyo, perched on a short ladder, was wiping sweat from his brow. A hammer dangled loosely from his right hand. From below, Naledi could see fresh nails shining amid the reeds and wood, a sure sign they'd used Otieno's supply. The sight made her chest glow with pride ; even if it was only half-finished, it looked sturdier than before.

"Hey, Boikonyo!" she called, shading her eyes with one hand. "Need any help?"

He glanced down, wearing his usual frown, but it seemed softer around the edges today. "I'm about done with this patch," he replied. "Mandla took off for school, said he'd come back. Could use an extra set of hands holding the ladder."

Naledi propped the ladder with both arms while Boikonyo tested the final nails, giving each a solid tap. Then he moved to descend, stepping carefully. When he reached the ground, he rolled his shoulders with a grunt of relief.

"Well," he said, wiping his brow with a rag. "That's half the roof done. Another couple of days, and the whole thing might not leak for a good while."

Naledi smiled. "It looks great. The nails are working, huh?"

A ghost of a smile touched Boikonyo's mouth. "They are. And that traveler Otieno gave us a fair price. You were right, you know ; sometimes these new folks passing through can be helpful."

Naledi blinked, momentarily surprised at her brother's admission. "I... yeah, I guess so."

He jerked his chin toward the hut's door. "Mama's inside, cooking up lunch. Go on. I'll wrap up out here." A moment later, he added, in a voice that almost sounded fatherly, "Thanks for helping with the ladder."

Naledi beamed. It wasn't a grand declaration of love, but for Boikonyo, those words meant a lot. She set the ladder firmly upright and went inside.

Zanele, her hair tied back with a printed scarf, stood over a simmering pot, stirring gently. The aroma of spiced beans and tomatoes filled the hut, making Naledi's stomach rumble. "How was school?" Zanele asked, glancing up.

"Good," Naledi replied, sliding onto a low stool. She recapped the highlights: Ms. Dlamini's interest in the polished spoon, their plan to approach more neighbors with scrap fixes, and Niya's notion of visiting Mr. Thema's storehouse. Zanele nodded along, a thoughtful look crossing her face.

"You children have a knack for picking up old metal and making it useful again," she mused. "But remember, if you promise to fix something, you'd better finish. Half-done repairs are worse than no repairs at all."

Naledi bristled a bit. "We know, Mama. We're taking it seriously. Mandla's good with the hammer, Niya's great with numbers, and I ; "

"You keep them in line," Zanele finished with a gentle laugh. "I know. And I'm proud of you all. It's just... well, be careful not to over-commit." A splash of concern flickered in her dark eyes. "Folks can be real demanding if they think you can fix everything."

Before Naledi could respond, Zanele ladled a portion of steaming beans into a shallow bowl and pushed it across the table. "Eat up, child, then you can go about your business. We'll see if we can sell some more fritters at the evening market."

Grateful, Naledi dug into her lunch, savoring each bite. The stew's tangy spices warmed her from within, matching the surge of excitement over the day's possibilities. While she ate, Zanele quietly bustled about, checking on dough rising in a covered bowl near the stove. The faint crackle of the thatched roof under Boikonyo's final taps was a comforting soundtrack ; a sign that, little by little, their home was growing sturdier.

Once she finished, Naledi thanked her mother and slipped outside again. Boikonyo had disappeared, likely gone to fetch more reeds or share a word with a neighbor. The yard was calm, the sun a bit lower in the sky, though the heat still pressed on her shoulders like a heavy blanket. She shielded her eyes, scanning the distance for Niya and Mandla, but they weren't in sight.

"Time to go," she told herself, patting the cloth bag at her side. A swirl of butterflies fluttered in her belly ; she'd see if Ms. Maseko had more hinges, or if Mr. Thema needed new spoons, or if Malume Nathi had a trove of interesting metal. Part of her hoped to catch a glimpse of Otieno and Hadzi again, maybe even the flute in that traveling chest ; though she tried to push that thought aside. No sense daydreaming when there was work to do.

She made her way to the Great Tree, where the day's brightness filtered through leaves in a patchwork of light and shade. She paused a moment upon arrival, resting a hand against the trunk. "Thank you," she whispered, a habit she'd formed for reasons she couldn't quite name ; gratitude, reverence, or just plain affection. The tree, as usual, only replied with a gentle shiver of leaves.

Niya was the first to appear, her basket dangling at her side.

"Naledi! Perfect timing." She jogged over, a sheen of sweat on her forehead. "Mandla's just behind me. We managed to talk Miss Maseko into letting us fix another pot she found in her storage. It's a bit banged up, but I think we can do it."

Naledi's eyes lit up. "That's great. And your talk with her was friendly?"

"More or less," Niya laughed. "She's still a bit prickly, but I think she respects our hustle."

Just then, Mandla showed up, lugging a burlap sack that clinked whenever he shifted. "This," he announced, hefting it with care, "is Miss Maseko's pot plus some random hinges she says are beyond salvage. We'll see about that."

Niya pointed at the sack. "Let's see if we can fix them tonight or early tomorrow. We can bring them to the next market, or maybe see if Ms. Dlamini wants them for the school building."

Naledi leaned in to examine the top of the pot poking through the sack. "Looks rusted, but not too bad," she commented. "If we can hammer out any dents, maybe patch up a hole or two…"

Mandla flashed a grin. "You read my mind."

They settled in a circle at the Great Tree's base, a rare patch of welcoming shade in an otherwise sweltering afternoon. Niya pulled out a rag and a small jar of polishing mix. Mandla arranged his hammer, a short chisel, and a battered piece of metal that served as an improvised anvil. Naledi took the burlap sack and gently laid out the items: a pot with a missing handle, two battered hinges, and a twisted spoon that looked more like a question mark than an eating utensil.

"All right," Niya said, "division of labor. Mandla, you tackle the pot first. Naledi, want to straighten that spoon and see if it's still usable? I'll try to file down the hinges. Then we'll rotate."

They nodded in agreement and got to work. Though the day

was hot, a breeze rustled through the branches every now and then, giving them small reprieves. The metallic clink of Mandla's hammer blended with Niya's soft scraping as she filed away rust, creating a steady, industrious rhythm. Naledi found a seat on a low root, pressing the twisted spoon against the improvised anvil. It took a few careful taps of a smaller hammer to coax the metal back into something that resembled cutlery.

"Got it," she muttered, wiping sweat from her brow, then testing the spoon's curve with her thumb. "Might not be perfectly straight, but it's definitely an improvement."

Mandla's pot was coming along, too; he'd managed to pry loose a rusted rivet and replace it with a small screw ; one of the spares he had salvaged from the last time Otieno passed through. Niya winced as a stubborn hinge refused to budge under her file. "This one's practically welded shut by rust," she grumbled. "But I can scrape it off if I keep at it."

They worked like that for a good hour, occasionally chatting about the next steps. Naledi mentioned Boikonyo's progress on the roof, making Mandla nod with satisfaction ; he'd help finish it tomorrow, he promised. Niya talked about her younger siblings, how they kept bugging her to teach them how to fix scraps too. Mandla cracked a joke about starting a "Scrap University," and that set them off laughing until their sides ached.

Eventually, the pot looked nearly presentable, the spoon almost straight, and one of the hinges was freed of rust enough to swivel. The second hinge might need more intense hammering, so Niya set it aside for later. By then, the sun had settled closer to the horizon, drenching the sky in orange and pink. A hush spread through the village as people finished the day's chores and looked forward to the evening meal.

Niya stretched, her back popping audibly. "Whew. That's enough for now. We can do the rest tomorrow before the market."

Mandla gathered the scraps carefully. "I'll keep them at my place for the night so they don't get lost. If Miss Maseko sees us making progress, she might pay a bit extra."

Naledi glanced up at the dappled sky visible through the leaves. "I should get home, too. Mama's probably done with the afternoon frying, and she'll want help cleaning or packing for the evening stall." But she hesitated, tapping her fingertips against the tree's bark. A part of her itched to share her secret wish about the flute. *Should I tell them how badly I want it?* she wondered, though they already had a sense. "Hey," she spoke up, "if we do well tomorrow, maybe I can stash a few coins away... for that flute."

Niya grinned broadly. "That's the plan. And hey, Mandla wants to buy a real hammer someday, so you're not the only one saving up. We all have dreams, Naledi."

Mandla gave a mock salute. "A real hammer, not these scraps. And maybe an actual anvil. Imagine how fast we could fix things then!"

Naledi breathed out a soft laugh. "All right, it's settled. We sell some scrap, put money toward what each of us wants. And maybe help out at home if needed."

They parted ways with high spirits. Niya and Mandla headed toward their respective huts, lugging the repaired items, while Naledi trod the path back to her own yard, cheeks still warm from the day's labor. Every so often, a gentle rustle overhead reminded her that the Great Tree watched on ; an ancient bystander to their small but hopeful endeavors.

She found Zanele out by the cooking station, wrapping fritters in banana leaves for easy carrying. Zanele looked up, nodded in greeting, and pointed to a small stack of dishes that needed washing. "How'd the scrap-fixing go?"

Naledi beamed. "Pretty well. We hammered out a pot for Miss

Maseko and saved a couple spoons, too. Gonna try to sell them soon."

Zanele's eyes softened, pride evident in her warm smile. "That's my girl," she said, handing Naledi a rag. "Could you clean these plates before the evening rush?"

Naledi nodded, rolling up her sleeves. "Sure thing, Mama." While she worked, her mind buzzed with the day's progress. Tomorrow might be a turning point ; if they sold enough, they'd be one step closer to their personal goals. *One step closer to the flute,* she added silently, her heart giving a small leap at the thought.

As she rinsed each plate, the yard's shadows lengthened, and the first hum of crickets began to fill the dusk. Boikonyo emerged from the hut, a tired set to his shoulders, but he managed a faint nod in Naledi's direction. They were all weary from a long day, yet the air crackled with a subdued energy, as if every one of them sensed that small changes were stacking up. The roof was half done, the scraps half sold, their hearts half hopeful. And maybe that was enough for now ; enough to keep them forging ahead.

Later, after the plates were set aside and the sun dipped below the horizon, Naledi stood once more at the edge of the yard, peering toward the silhouette of the Great Tree. In the hush of twilight, she couldn't see the leaves in detail ; just a broad outline rising tall against a sky of deepening violet. But she felt its presence, steady as a heartbeat.

"Goodnight," she whispered, though no one else was around to hear. And as she turned back to help Zanele with closing chores, she carried within her the hush of that ancient giant, a hush brimming with possibilities for tomorrow and all the tomorrows to come.

GIFTS OF GENEROSITY, ECHOES OF SONG

Bright and early the next morning, Naledi awoke to the familiar clatter of pots and the smell of frying dough drifting through the hut. She blinked away the remnants of sleep, pulling herself upright on her thin mat. Outside, roosters crowed an off-key choir, signaling the village to rise. Once again, her family was up before dawn, each with some pressing task in mind.

She slipped on her sandals, already feeling the day's warmth edging in through the small window. From the way Zanele's stirring spoon scraped against the pot, Naledi guessed her mother was making fresh fritters ; no doubt for the market that afternoon. Naledi's stomach fluttered with excitement. *Today's the day,* she thought, remembering how she, Niya, and Mandla planned to sell their repaired items. *Our first real test.*

Stepping into the main room, she found Zanele by the stove, hair tied back in a neat scarf. Over on the other side of the hut, Boikonyo adjusted the last of the thatch patch he'd brought inside to keep dry. A faint, earthy smell of freshly cut reeds mingled with the mouthwatering aroma of frying batter. The hut felt cramped with all these supplies, but somehow cozy, too.

"Morning, Mama," Naledi said, voice still scratchy. "Can I help?"

Zanele turned to greet her, offering a soft smile. "Morning, child. If you'd fetch me some water from the jug, that'd be a blessing. These fritters are nearly done." She nodded at the clay jug near the door. "Then we'll talk about your big day."

Naledi's heart skipped. "Yes, Mama!" She hurried to the jug, pouring a small cupful of water for her mother, careful not to spill. As she handed it over, she caught Boikonyo's eye. He grunted what might've been a greeting, then returned his attention to the reeds.

"How's the roof?" she asked him, trying to keep her tone light.

He shrugged. "Mostly stable. I've got Mandla coming by later to nail down a few loose spots. You'll see ; one good rain, and we won't have a drop inside."

Naledi couldn't hide her grin. "That's great. Thank you."

A low chuckle rumbled in his throat ; Boikonyo's way of acknowledging her gratitude. Then he rose to set the reeds aside. "Going to gather some scraps for Mandla. Says he needs more metal shards for patching that old kettle if he wants to sell it."

Zanele turned off the stove, transferring the fresh batch of fritters onto a waiting tray. Steam curled upward, carrying the fragrance of spiced dough. "The rest of these are for the market," she told Naledi, "though we can spare a few to nibble on. Eat quickly, though. You've got a big day ahead, right?"

Naledi nodded, helping herself to a warm fritter. A pleasant hush settled as she chewed, the crisp outside giving way to soft, flavorful dough. She nearly hummed with delight. Zanele poured herself a small cup of tea, then handed Naledi one as well, letting them share a companionable moment before the day's rush.

"So," Zanele said, easing onto a low stool, "Niya and Mandla are meeting you under the Great Tree?"

Naledi swallowed her last bite. "Yes. We'll gather our repaired items. Then we'll go to the market ; maybe we'll set up a small corner near your stall if there's room."

Zanele tapped her chin thoughtfully. "We usually have visitors and locals wandering in all afternoon. Plenty of potential buyers." She glanced at Boikonyo, who was fussing with a bit of thatch. "Might want to place yourselves close to other vendors, so folks can see what you're offering."

"I will," Naledi promised. "We've got spoons, a kettle, some hinges ; stuff that can be reused. Maybe Ms. Dlamini will drop by if she's free, or others from the school."

Zanele's expression softened. "You've done well, child. And your brother's starting to come around to these travelers ; he sees the good in new ideas, even if he won't say it outright."

Naledi felt a warmth spread in her chest. "I just hope we do enough business to prove we're serious. I don't want folks thinking we're just playing around."

With a gentle nod, Zanele stood and offered Naledi one more fritter. "Don't fret too much. You've worked hard, and people see that. Now, get going before the sun climbs any higher."

Naledi popped the last fritter into her mouth and rushed outside. The day was already bright ; rays of yellow light angled across the yard, creating long shadows from the hut and a half-finished woodpile. She paused to take in the sight of their patched roof, feeling a proud twinge at how the nails had done their job, then headed off toward the Great Tree.

A modest crowd had gathered near the village center for the market, though the event wouldn't peak until closer to midday. Stalls and tables were set up in a loose semicircle, each displaying vegetables, handwoven goods, or small homemade treats. People milled about, greeting neighbors and exchanging coins with idle chatter.

When Naledi arrived at the Great Tree, Niya was already there, her wire basket propped against a thick root. Mandla trudged up moments later, cradling an old tin kettle in one arm and a cloth bundle tucked under the other. They exchanged excited smiles, each weighed down by the fruit of their labors.

"Morning!" Niya called, waving Naledi over. "We're set, I think. Mandla's hammered the kettle one last time, and I finished polishing these spoons." She tapped the basket, revealing the shiny utensils wrapped in cloth for protection.

"Looks good," Naledi remarked, peering in. Everything had a neat, refurbished gleam, though some items still bore minor imperfections. "We'll see who's willing to buy."

Mandla set his cloth bundle on the root to reveal a few hinges that still looked a bit rough, but workable. "If we can't sell them as is, we'll at least advertise our repair services," he said, rubbing the back of his neck. "No point letting them gather dust again."

"Right," Niya agreed. "Let's find a spot near Zanele's stall, so folks who come for fritters might see our stuff, too."

They hoisted their items and trekked toward the cluster of stalls. Zanele waved them over to an empty patch of ground not far from her table, where the scent of spiced dough mingled with the earthy aroma of newly arrived produce. They laid out a scrap of cloth to set their wares on, each piece displayed in neat rows. Niya's wire basket sat off to the side, ready to hold any coins they might earn.

Naledi couldn't help but glance around, searching for the bright wagon of Otieno and Hadzi. She spotted it near the far end, where a small group of curious onlookers had gathered to examine the travelers' wares. A flicker of excitement rose in

Naledi's chest ; she remembered the bamboo flute, shining in that painted chest, calling to her heart. She swallowed, forcing herself to focus on the present. *We've got to earn some coins first.*

"Okay," Niya said, hands on her hips. "I'll handle the money and keep track of sales. Mandla, you can explain the repairs if people have questions. Naledi, you greet them ; make sure they know we're friendly, yeah?"

Naledi grinned. "Got it." She felt an odd rush, like stepping onto a small stage with an eager audience. *Though it's just a dusty patch of ground,* she told herself, *our shop is real.*

At first, no one stopped by ; folks were drawn to the more established stalls, picking up fresh tomatoes or haggling over chili peppers. But gradually, a middle-aged man approached, eyeing the kettle with a skeptical look. Naledi stepped forward, offering her best smile.

"Morning, sir," she said politely. "We fix metal scraps ; pots, spoons, whatever needs mending. This kettle used to be bent and leaky, but we patched it up. Pretty sturdy now."

He lifted the kettle, tapping its side. Mandla gave a quick rundown of how he hammered out the dents and sealed the hole. The man asked for the price, and Niya stated it clearly. After a moment of haggling and curious prodding, the man nodded. "All right," he said. "I'll take it. My old kettle's about done for anyway."

Niya grinned as she accepted the few coins he handed over. "Pleasure doing business with you," she beamed. "Come back if you need anything else repaired."

The man walked off, cradling his new kettle like a small victory. The trio exchanged looks of triumph, Niya tucking the coins into her wire basket with a satisfied clink. Naledi felt her pulse quicken ; this was their first genuine sale to someone outside their immediate circle.

Not long after, an older woman ambled over, drawn by the gleaming spoons. She sniffed as though uncertain, but Niya's bright manner soon won her interest. "We can sell you one or two, or fix your existing cutlery," Niya offered. "Whichever suits you best."

The woman eventually bought two spoons, parting with a couple of coins. Naledi's heart soared again. *That's more progress.* She stole a glance across the market, glimpsing Zanele's proud smile from where she sold fritters. Even Boikonyo hung around the edges, arms crossed, but a faint grin tugged at the corners of his mouth. He gave Naledi a small nod.

As midday approached, the market bustled with new energy. A few people asked about the hinges, though no one bought them just yet. Niya and Mandla fielded questions about repairing everything from cracked ladles to warped pans. Naledi took note of potential orders, scrawling them in a small notebook to follow up later. In the swirl of activity, she felt more alive than ever ; like she was part of something that mattered, an enterprise that brought a spark of possibility to the dusty village.

Eventually, a brief lull settled on their corner of the market. Naledi wiped her brow with the back of her hand. "Whew," she breathed, glancing at Niya's wire basket. "We've done... all right."

Niya nodded, peeking at the coin count. "We might have enough for you to buy half that flute," she teased, elbowing Naledi. "If you chip in your share, and Mandla wants to chip in, maybe the travelers would let you do partial payment."

Naledi's heart somersaulted. She gazed toward Otieno and Hadzi's wagon, where a handful of villagers now examined fabric rolls. "Should I... should I ask?" she whispered, nerves coiling in her stomach.

"Why not?" Mandla replied, shrugging. "We can watch the stall for a minute, if you want to go talk to them. No harm in trying, right?"

Taking a steadying breath, Naledi nodded, handing Niya the small notebook. "I'll be back soon. Just keep an eye out for anyone wanting repairs."

She weaved through the throng, slipping past stalls of stacked vegetables and woven baskets. Closer to Otieno's wagon, the chatter grew louder, folks admiring fabrics or small wooden carvings. Hadzi stood on one side, laughing with a woman who seemed enchanted by a carved elephant figurine.

Naledi approached carefully, waiting for an opening in the bustle. Otieno noticed her first, smiling in recognition. "Hello there," he greeted, tipping his hat. "How's your morning going? Any luck with the scraps you kids fix?"

She mustered a grin. "We sold a kettle and a couple spoons, actually. It's going well." She paused, fiddling with the hem of her skirt. "And, um… I wanted to ask you about something." Her gaze slid to the painted chest in the back of the wagon ; where the flutes likely lay.

Otieno followed her eyes, nodding knowingly. "Ah, the instruments, right? I remember you took a fancy to one of those bamboo flutes."

Naledi's cheeks warmed. "Yes. I… I don't have all the money for it, but I have a bit. And if we keep selling more scraps, I could pay the rest soon. Would… that be possible?"

Hadzi turned from her conversation, tipping her head to eavesdrop. She gave Naledi a friendly smile. "We're open to layaway deals," she said, voice carrying a hint of humor. "As long as we're in the village another few days, anyway. We'll want the full price before we move on."

Naledi's heart fluttered. "That would be wonderful. I'll pay some now, and hopefully the rest by the time you leave. How much is it again?"

Hadzi glanced at Otieno, who pulled a small ledger from under the wagon seat. He flipped to a page and read out the cost ; higher than Naledi had hoped, but not impossible. She swallowed, mentally counting the coins Niya carried from their morning sales.

"I think I can pay half today," she offered, voice trembling with both nerves and hope. "I'll get the rest as soon as more scraps sell."

Otieno snapped the ledger shut. "Fair enough." Then he rummaged in the painted chest, pulling out a bamboo flute with intricate carvings swirling near the mouthpiece. He held it out carefully. "This the one?"

Naledi's breath caught. The flute's smooth finish glistened under the midday sun, the carvings seeming to dance along its length. She reached out, hands steady despite her pounding pulse. *Yes, it's perfect.* She nodded, speechless for a moment.

"So," Hadzi said, crossing her arms, "you give us half now, and we hold on to it until you're ready to pay the rest. But maybe we can let you try a few notes?" She winked. "Just a sample, to keep that spark alive."

Naledi, cheeks burning with excitement, handed over the coins she had in her pouch ; a portion from her share of the scrap earnings plus a small stash she'd saved from helping Zanele in the past. Then Otieno offered her the flute, though he kept a gentle grip on the end. "Go on," he encouraged, "play us a tune."

She raised it to her lips, heart hammering so loud she wondered if they could hear it. The wind parted around her mouth, and she blew gently. At first, only a faint breathy sound emerged, like air through a hollow tube. But on her second attempt, a clear note rang out ; soft, high, and sweet as a birdcall at dawn. Naledi's entire body tingled, every nerve alive with a feeling she couldn't quite name.

Hadzi laughed, clapping her hands. "Not bad for a beginner."

Otieno nodded in approval. "That's a fine start."

The note faded, and Naledi lowered the flute, breathless. She wanted nothing more than to keep playing, but she remembered she still owed them the other half of the payment. Reluctantly, she passed it back.

Hadzi accepted it with care, tucking it back into the painted chest. "It'll wait for you," she said gently. "Don't tarry too long, though. We might pack up and go in a few days."

"I won't," Naledi promised. She felt like she was floating. "Thank you."

Otieno nodded. "Good luck, little scrap-fixer. Hope you sell enough to get your music."

With her heart soaring, Naledi made her way back to Niya and Mandla. They eyed her with curiosity, and she barely managed to contain her giddy grin. "They're letting me pay half now, half later," she blurted, practically bouncing on her toes. "I can't take it yet, but I got to play one note. It… it was beautiful."

Niya laughed, hugging Naledi with one arm. "That's amazing!"

Mandla gave her a playful nudge. "Then we'd better keep selling, so you can cover the rest. Let's see if we can't snag a few more customers."

The trio re-focused on their makeshift stall, energy renewed by Naledi's small victory. It didn't matter if the sun beat down or if some villagers passed by without a glance. They felt unstoppable. Every coin they earned, every pot they polished, carried them closer to their dreams ; be it a flute, a real hammer, or just enough capital to keep the scrap shop afloat.

And so the day wore on, filled with conversations, curious

buyers, and the thrill of enterprise. By late afternoon, they had sold another spoon and taken orders for two more repairs. Niya beamed at the growing pile of coins, Mandla mused about taking on bigger items soon, and Naledi's thoughts drifted to the sweet, single note she'd coaxed from that flute.

When the market finally began winding down, the sun dipped low behind the huts, casting shadows that stretched across the dusty ground. Naledi packed up the few unsold pieces, and Niya carefully tallied their day's earnings. Mandla, yawning, said he'd drop the leftover scraps at his place before nightfall. Everyone felt tired, but it was the satisfying kind of tired, like a reward for a job well done.

As Naledi helped her mother close up the fritter stall, she cast one last look at Otieno and Hadzi's wagon. It glowed faintly in the twilight, as though lit by an inner lantern. *I'll be back,* she thought fiercely. *I'll get the rest of those coins, and that flute will be mine.*

She caught a glimpse of the Great Tree at the edge of her vision, leaves rustling in the evening breeze. A wave of gratitude swelled in her chest ; gratitude for the patch in the roof, for the coins jingling in Niya's basket, for Mandla's hammer and Boikonyo's newly softened scowl, for Zanele's quiet smile of pride. And yes, for the single note on that bamboo flute that echoed in her mind like a promise.

The day ended with tired feet and hopeful hearts. As darkness gathered and the village settled into a lull, Naledi went to bed, hugging the memory of that note to her like a warm blanket. Outside, the Great Tree stood silent in the moonlight, bearing witness to a world in which dreams ; small as flutes or as grand as the sky ; could slip closer to reality, one coin at a time.

TWILIGHT GAMES AND UNSPOKEN NOTES

The day after Naledi played her first trembling note on the bamboo flute, the village stirred awake under an overcast sky. Thin clouds drifted across the early sun, lending the usual orange glow a muted, grayish tint. It wasn't quite threatening rain, but it had the feel of a day poised between sunshine and storms ; as if the world couldn't decide which way to lean.

Naledi rose at first light, her heart still dancing with the memory of that flute's single, pure tone. Though she didn't yet have enough coins to bring it home, the promise of returning to Otieno and Hadzi with the remainder spurred her into motion. If she had to fix broken hinges and polish dented spoons all day, so be it. She'd come this far ; surely she could go a bit further.

She found Zanele at the fire pit outside the hut, stirring a small pot of porridge. "Morning, Mama," she said, rubbing sleep from her eyes.

Zanele greeted her with a gentle smile. "Morning, child. You're up early again. Thinking about that flute, aren't you?"

Naledi's cheeks warmed. "A little," she admitted. "But I also want to see how Niya and Mandla are doing with the new scraps. We promised to keep going, right?"

Zanele chuckled. "You've got the spirit of a trader, Naledi. Your father ; " She paused, stirring the porridge with renewed focus, as though she'd said more than she meant to. "Well, never mind. Let's just say he would've been proud to see you so determined."

A strange tug of longing caught at Naledi's chest. Her father was rarely spoken of, so even a small mention, a hint of who he'd been, felt like a precious gift. She swallowed. "Thank you, Mama."

"Here," Zanele said, ladling a portion of porridge into a wooden bowl and passing it over. "Eat up. You'll need your strength if you're spending the day chasing after broken metal."

Naledi took the bowl, savoring the simple warmth of each spoonful. The day's light was brightening in a faint, diffused way, as if behind a curtain. Over at the side of the hut, Boikonyo emerged from inside, arms loaded with leftover thatch. At the sight of Naledi, he gave a small grunt that might've been a greeting.

"Going to reinforce that corner of the roof," he said, nodding at the hut. "Storm might come eventually. Don't want to be caught off guard."

Naledi swallowed a spoonful of porridge and gave him a thumbs-up. "You need Mandla's help?"

Boikonyo shrugged. "If he's around, sure. If not, I'll manage. Just let him know."

A hush passed between them ; simple, unspoken understanding ; before Boikonyo moved on to his work. Naledi finished her breakfast, thanked Zanele, and headed off to find her friends.

The Great Tree stood in quiet majesty despite the dim sky. Its broad branches stirred in the mild breeze, leaves whispering like a half-forgotten lullaby. Naledi spotted Niya first, perched on a root so big she could have used it as a seat. She was sorting through a small pouch of coins with a thoughtful frown. Mandla crouched nearby, tinkering with a short piece of twisted wire that looked like it might become a makeshift handle.

"Morning," Naledi called, lifting a hand in greeting.

Niya glanced up, nodding with a half-smile. "Morning, Naledi. You're just in time ; Mandla's trying to fix a broken ladle handle for Miss Maseko, but the wire's not bending right."

Mandla grunted, holding up the wire. "I'll get it, just need to heat it or hammer it better. We can't waste a chunk of good metal on a small job if wire will do."

Naledi set her cloth bag aside. "Mind if I watch?" she asked. "I can run errands if you need me to fetch a tool."

Mandla shrugged, handing her the wire. "Feel free to try bending this. My hands are cramping. We might need the small pliers from my place."

Niya clicked her tongue. "And we might have bigger fish to fry soon. Mr. Thema asked if we could fix a large cooking pot for his storehouse. It's got a hole near the bottom and a busted handle."

Naledi's eyes widened. "That sounds like real work. He's usually picky about quality, too. If we do it wrong, he'll tell everyone."

"All the more reason to do it right," Mandla said, flashing a determined grin.

They spent a few minutes discussing the pot, how best to patch a hole without the right solder or specialized tools. Niya suggested layering thin scrap metal, Mandla wanted to try a rivet. Naledi, remembering Zanele's caution, said, "We should be sure we can finish the job before we promise a delivery date. If we're in over our heads, folks might lose faith in us."

Niya nodded thoughtfully. "Agreed. Let's see how the smaller repairs go first. We've got the hinges and ladle for Miss Maseko, plus a pan Ms. Dlamini wants patched. If we handle those well, then Mr. Thema might trust us with something bigger."

Mandla set aside the troublesome wire. "So we do these small tasks first, then talk to Mr. Thema. Good plan."

They divvied up tasks ; Niya would handle hinges, Mandla the pan, and Naledi the ladle. Once they'd hammered out the final shape, they'd decide on next steps for the big pot job. Before they could start, though, Niya glanced at the sky. "I might run home for a moment, grab the small hammer I left behind. The one with the flatter head. Be right back."

As Niya jogged off, Mandla turned to Naledi. "You want to try bending that wire? I've got the pliers in my bag. My fingers are numb."

She nodded, taking the pliers he offered. "Sure, but if I break it, don't blame me."

Mandla chuckled. "Better broken now than halfway through the repair."

So Naledi set to work, carefully coaxing the wire into a curved shape that could fit around the ladle's broken stub. Her arms strained, but she kept a steady pressure. The overcast sky deepened, making the morning feel oddly subdued, as if the village itself was waiting for something ; rain, news, or a new tune to break the hush.

After a few minutes, Naledi managed a decent curve. "Hey, Mandla, think this'll do?" she asked, raising the wire for inspection.

He peered at it and nodded. "Not bad. Let's see if we can attach it to the ladle. Then we can secure it with a quick twist of that leftover bit of metal."

They worked side by side, the clink of metal echoing beneath the Great Tree. The leaves stirred in a breeze that carried the distant scent of coming rain. Naledi's mind wandered briefly to the flute, how that single note lingered in her memory like a promise waiting to be fulfilled. *Focus on the ladle,* she scolded herself gently. *Music will come later.*

Niya returned a short while later, small hammer in hand. "Got it," she announced. "Plus a bit of leftover polish, in case we need to shine anything up."

With renewed vigor, they fell into an easy rhythm ; hammering, bending, filing. Occasionally, a villager passed by, curious about their progress. One woman paused to say she had a broken spatula at home; Niya jotted down her name in a small notebook. Another man asked if they could eventually fix a metal bucket for watering livestock. Mandla said, "Sure, next week ; if the price is right." The man chuckled, evidently pleased.

The morning slipped by this way, the three friends hunched over their makeshift workstation, the Great Tree's shade cool against the rising warmth. Around midday, they finally tested the ladle's new handle, dipping it into a bucket of water Niya had brought. The wire held firm, no leaks or wiggles. Naledi grinned. "Looks like Miss Maseko will get a working ladle after all."

Mandla flexed his fingers. "Now let's see about Ms. Dlamini's pan."

They turned their attention to the next item ; a small frying pan with a crack along the edge. Niya tapped the crack with her hammer, trying to see if it could be patched with a small metal strip. As Mandla prepared a piece of scrap metal, Naledi took a moment to stand and stretch, scanning the village around them.

Movement caught her eye. At the far end of the lane stood Otieno and Hadzi's wagon, the one that held the flute. A pang of urgency struck her ; *Hadzi said they wouldn't stay forever.* She resolved to check on how many more coins they needed after finishing these repairs. Perhaps, if they sold the ladle and Ms. Dlamini's pan quickly, she could scrape together enough to finalize the flute payment.

She knelt again, helping Niya hold the pan steady while Mandla positioned the scrap piece over the crack. "Steady…" he muttered, tapping small rivets through the metal and into the pan's edge. It took several tries, a few curses under breath, and a final, resounding strike of the hammer, but eventually, the patch held. Niya's polishing rag came next, buffing away rough edges. By the time they finished, the old pan gleamed with renewed life.

"Yes!" Niya said, pumping her fist softly. "I can't wait to show Ms. Dlamini."

Mandla nodded, wiping sweat from his forehead. "Let's gather everything. We'll deliver Miss Maseko's ladle and Ms. Dlamini's pan. With luck, they'll pay on the spot."

Naledi felt a swell of hope. "Then maybe we can talk to Mr. Thema about the big pot. And if that goes well, I might have my flute money."

Niya shot her a supportive grin. "Exactly. Let's move."

They walked through the dusty lanes in the mild afternoon, items in hand. Niya carried the ladle carefully, as if it were a precious artifact, while Naledi held the pan wrapped in cloth. Mandla lagged slightly behind, rummaging in his satchel for scraps of wire or rivets in case their customers asked for last-minute tweaks. The sky remained overcast, the sun hidden behind a thickening layer of cloud.

At Miss Maseko's hut ; a structure that leaned as if listening to the ground ; they found the old woman seated on a stool, half-dozing with a cat sprawled at her feet. She snapped awake at their approach, eyes narrowing until she recognized them.

"Ah, the fix-it crew," she said, her voice gravelly with age. "Got my ladle?"

Niya stepped forward, smiling confidently. "Repaired and ready." She handed over the ladle. "We replaced the broken handle with wire, hammered it snug. Should hold fine now."

Miss Maseko scrutinized it, tugging on the wire a few times and squinting at the joint. The cat meowed disinterestedly, twisting about before plopping back to sleep. After a tense moment, the old woman gave a curt nod. "Looks solid. I suppose I owe you something for that."

Niya mentioned a small price they'd agreed upon earlier, and Miss Maseko grumbled about "prices these days" but fished out a few coins from a pocket in her skirt. She dropped them into Niya's open palm, and the clink of metal made Naledi's heart flutter.

"Thank you," Mandla said politely. "If there's anything else ; "

Miss Maseko waved him off. "We'll see." But her eyes weren't unkind; she patted the ladle as though it were an old friend reunited. "Go on, then."

Off they went, coins nestled safely in Niya's wire basket. Next stop: Ms. Dlamini's place. Although she was the schoolteacher, she boarded in a modest hut near the center of the village. They found her sorting through a small stack of books by a rickety wooden table out front.

"Afternoon, Ms. Dlamini," Naledi greeted, carefully unwrapping the frying pan. "We finished patching this. No more cracks. Mandla riveted it."

Ms. Dlamini peered at the pan, impressed by its sturdy patch. She tapped it lightly, satisfied with the sound. "Nicely done," she acknowledged. "We could use this for the school's lunches or a cooking lesson. How much did we agree on?"

Niya quoted the price. Ms. Dlamini nodded. "Fair." She handed over coins, then turned the pan this way and that, as if admiring how new it looked compared to the battered mess she'd given them.

"You keep surprising me, children," she added, tone warm with a trace of humor. "But don't forget your lessons, eh? Real success takes a sharp mind."

Mandla grinned. "We won't forget, ma'am."

As they left, Niya and Naledi counted the coins in the basket ; a decent sum for the day's efforts. Mandla rifled through them, eyes alight. "We might be able to afford that pot repair for Mr. Thema's storehouse ; buy the rivets we need," he reasoned. "And maybe that'll bring in even more money."

Naledi nodded, heart thrumming with excitement. *More money, more chance to buy the flute.* She scanned the horizon. Late afternoon was edging in, the clouds thickening overhead. "Should we go talk to Mr. Thema now?" she asked.

Niya hesitated, glancing at the sky. "Might be a storm. We can at least see if he's free. Let's hurry."

They walked briskly, heading for Mr. Thema's storehouse near the far side of the village. The building stood taller than most huts, made of sturdier timbers and wide doors for storing grain or goods. A small group of people milled about, talking in hushed tones, and among them, Naledi spotted Boikonyo. He caught sight of her and gestured with his head, as if beckoning them over.

"What's going on?" Niya asked, picking up her pace.

Boikonyo's brow was furrowed in concern. "Rumor is, a messenger just rode in from a neighboring village," he said. "They're expecting heavy rains soon, maybe a storm that'll blow this way in a day or two. Folks are worried about their roofs, storehouses, everything."

Mandla's eyes widened. "Guess we picked a good time to fix metal scraps."

Boikonyo nodded, though he didn't smile. "Yeah. People might need pots, hinges for shutters, all that. But be careful ; when storms come, people also get desperate. They might demand repairs on short notice, get angry if you can't do them fast."

Naledi swallowed, thinking of Mr. Thema's big pot. Would he insist on immediate repairs? And what about the flute ; would Otieno and Hadzi leave sooner if the weather turned foul? The day felt suddenly tight, time closing in around them.

Niya exchanged a look with Naledi, then turned to Boikonyo. "We'll do our best, but we need to be honest about what we can fix in time."

"That's wise," Boikonyo agreed, glancing at Naledi. Something in his face seemed… gentler. "Better to do that than promise the moon and deliver a rock."

"Thanks," Naledi murmured, surprised by his advice.

Just then, Mr. Thema emerged from the storehouse, a heavyset man with a commanding presence. He paused, noticing the small group. "Oh, it's you children," he said, voice booming. "Heard you're mending metal scraps. I've got a big pot with a hole near the bottom ; needs to be watertight, or my grains might go bad if water seeps in." He gestured impatiently. "Think you can handle it before the rains come?"

Niya lifted her chin, speaking with careful confidence. "We can try. We'll look at the damage first, then see if we have enough rivets and metal. If we can't do it well, we'll tell you."

Mr. Thema squinted, sizing them up. Finally, he nodded curtly. "Fair enough. Come inside."

Mandla, Niya, and Naledi followed him into the storehouse, while Boikonyo lingered outside with the messenger and other villagers. Inside, the smell of dried grains and dusty corners filled the dim space. Stacks of sacks lined the walls, and in the middle of the floor lay the pot in question; large and iron-walled, sporting a ragged hole on one side.

Niya and Mandla knelt to inspect it, tapping the metal to judge its thickness. Naledi hovered anxiously, mindful of the thickening clouds outside. *If we fix this quickly, maybe we'll earn enough to buy the flute and help folks prep for the storm.*

She caught Niya's eye, who gave a small nod. "We'll do our best," Niya whispered. Naledi nodded back, heart set on the challenge. The day might bring storms of wind and rain, but for now, the hush of approaching weather only steeled her resolve. If they succeeded here, she could finalize payment for that precious flute ; her father's unspoken legacy tugging at her heart ; and maybe, just maybe, play more than a single note, weaving a gentle melody through the troubled air before the storm broke.

"I know," Naledi said, voice small. "But Otieno and Hadzi could leave anytime if the storm's too big."

Mandla slung his tool bag over his shoulder. "Let's head back to the Great Tree, count what we have, and decide. We should also plan how to handle new repairs if the storm hits. People might panic."

Niya nodded. "Agreed. Storm or no storm, we better not lose track of what we've earned."

They retraced their steps through the village, the air growing heavy with an electric charge. A few drops of rain splattered here and there, though not yet enough to call it a shower. Neighbors hurried to tie down loose items in their yards, and a few goats wandered frantically, sensing the change in weather. Naledi felt a mixture of excitement and anxiety swirl in her chest.

Under the Great Tree's canopy, the wind rustled leaves in a low murmur. The trio settled on a broad root, Niya emptying her coin pouch onto a folded cloth. Together, they sorted and counted: the ladle job, Ms. Dlamini's pan, Mr. Thema's pot, plus leftover scraps. After subtracting the cost of rivets and small bits of wire, Niya tallied up their net earnings.

"All right," she said at last, eyes bright. "We've actually done well. Enough for each of us to save a bit. If we keep a little for future materials, we can still split the remainder three ways. And that might cover your flute, Naledi."

Naledi's heart soared. "Are you sure? I don't want to short the business."

Mandla grinned. "We're good. We can always earn more if folks keep needing repairs. You better get that flute before the storm chases Otieno and Hadzi away."

Niya pressed the coins into Naledi's hands. They felt warm and reassuring, like a promise made real. She glanced at the sky, the wind tugging at her hair. "I'll go now," she said, jumping to her feet. "Might not have another chance."

"I'll pack up here," Mandla said, gesturing to the rivets and tools. "Take Niya's basket so the coins don't go jingling everywhere. We'll see you at your hut or maybe the market if you're lucky."

GATHERING STORMS, SILENT MELODIES

If there was one thing that could rattle even the most steadfast folk in Naledi's village, it was the threat of a storm rolling in uninvited, set on lashing rooftops and drenching the dusty paths until they turned to thick mud. Word had trickled in that morning ; via a weary messenger from a neighboring settlement ; that heavy rains were on their way, possibly dragging thunder and gusting winds behind them. By midday, everyone was abuzz with that special mix of excitement and dread storms always bring.

Naledi felt the tremor of anticipation, too, but it didn't wholly drown out her own pressing thoughts: the battered pot Mr. Thema wanted repaired, the flute she still owed money on, and the patch of roof at home that might still be vulnerable if the wind howled enough. She couldn't let herself dwell too long on each worry ; there was simply too much to do.

They began inside Mr. Thema's storehouse, a tall building smelling of dry grain and sawdust. Niya and Mandla crouched around the giant iron pot, their heads nearly touching as they inspected the ragged hole near its bottom. Naledi hovered nearby, arms folded, scanning the dim corners of the storehouse. Stacks of burlap sacks loomed in shadows, and a single lantern flickered overhead.

Mr. Thema stood behind them, arms folded. He was a large man, not just in girth but in the way he carried himself; like any room he entered became his by default. He watched the three with something between impatience and concern. After all, water and grain didn't mix well, and a pot that leaked could mean a spoiled harvest.

"Well?" Mr. Thema asked gruffly. "You see a way to patch it, or must I find someone else?"

Niya cleared her throat and spoke in that calm, measured way she'd perfected when dealing with grown-ups. "We think we can do it. The metal around the hole's not too thin; just rusted. With a riveted patch, we can make it watertight again."

Mandla nodded, tapping the pot with a small hammer. "We'll need enough rivets, though, plus a piece of iron to cover the hole. We can shape it to match the curve. Should hold unless the storm's a real monster."

Mr. Thema's frown deepened. "Better hold under a real monster, because that's exactly what folks are saying is coming."

Naledi swallowed, remembering how windy storms could rip off even sturdy roofs or flood entire huts if the downpour lasted. "We'll do our best," she assured him. "But we'll have to work fast. Mind if we move the pot somewhere with better light?"

He shrugged, stepping aside. "Sure. But be careful not to dent it further. That pot's older than me."

Mandla suppressed a grin; *older than Mr. Thema* might well be ancient indeed. "We'll be careful," he promised. "Niya, can you help me lug this outside, near the doorway?"

Niya grabbed one side, Mandla the other. The pot was heavy but not impossible to lift together. Naledi trotted ahead, pushing the broad doors open wide so a shaft of midday light streamed into the storehouse. Outside, the wind stirred dust in small spirals, and the sky still wore that sullen, gray look, as though an argument was brewing beyond the horizon.

Once they set the pot down on a sturdy wooden crate just outside, Niya and Mandla paused to catch their breath. Naledi stepped close. "So what now?" she asked quietly.

"Now we see if we can measure the hole and figure out what scrap metal we need," Niya said. "We'll take some notes, maybe run to Mandla's stash or Malume Nathi's shop, see if we have a piece that fits. Then we rivet it. Sound good?"

Mandla nodded, wiping the back of his neck with a cloth. "Yeah. And we might need your help holding things in place, Naledi. Could be a three-person job."

She agreed, and the trio busied themselves, measuring the hole's diameter. Niya used a scrap of chalk to mark approximate lines around the ragged edges. All the while, Mr. Thema hovered a few steps away, arms still crossed, eyes flicking up to the darkening sky as if daring the storm to come early.

"We'll be as quick as we can," Naledi assured him.

He just grunted. "No dawdling. If those clouds burst before my grain's safe, I'll regret trusting children to do a man's job."

Naledi bristled, but Niya's hand on her arm kept her calm. "We understand," Niya said diplomatically. "We'll show you it's not a mistake."

With that, they scurried off to gather supplies. Mandla darted to Malume Nathi's shop, hoping the old shopkeeper might have a discarded iron plate sturdy enough to serve as a patch. Niya and Naledi jogged back to Mandla's hut, rummaging through a bin of leftover scrap to find rivets, washers, and any extra wire that might be useful.

When they reconvened at the storehouse door, Mandla held aloft a chunk of iron about the size of his open palm. "Malume Nathi says it was part of an old cooking stove. Should match the pot's thickness pretty well."

"Perfect," Niya said, giving it a quick inspection. "We can shape it if needed. Let's see if the curve matches."

Mr. Thema looked on, still skeptical but no longer interrupting. With care, Mandla pressed the patch against the pot's hole. There was a small gap on one edge, but the curve was close enough. "We'll hammer that edge a bit to shape it," he murmured. Naledi handed him a small mallet, and he tapped steadily, the clang reverberating through the dusty air.

Niya organized the rivets in a neat row. "We'll line them around the patch, maybe five or six should hold it. Naledi, can you heat one corner of that patch with the portable brazier?"

Naledi nodded, moving to the small charcoal brazier Niya had brought from home. She used a piece of cloth to hold the metal and directed the patch near the coals, letting the heat soften it enough for Mandla to tap it into shape. Beads of sweat trickled down Naledi's forehead ; partly from the heat, partly from the ever-present tension of beating the storm's arrival.

With the patch warmed, Mandla hammered gently, Niya sliding rivets through the holes. Naledi used the pliers to bend the rivets inside the pot, flattening them against metal washers. It was meticulous work, each clang of the mallet a fresh test of their patience.

"All right," Niya said after a few minutes, stepping back. "Let's see if we've got it sealed."

They hoisted the pot upright, Naledi steadying it while Mandla poured in a bucket of water from the well. For a tense moment, all four of them ; including Mr. Thema ; watched to see if water would trickle out. The water level remained steady. A tiny bead of moisture formed at one seam, but it didn't run ; just clung there as if uncertain whether to leak or not.

"That looks… decent," Mandla ventured, letting out a breath.

Mr. Thema knelt, running a calloused finger along the rivets. "You call that a patch?" he asked, gruffness intact. But Naledi detected a note of grudging admiration in his tone. "No real drips, I see."

Niya cleared her throat. "It might drip a little at first, especially if the pot gets banged around. But if you keep it upright and treat it gently, it should hold water through any storm."

"Might want to wipe a bit of tar on the seam from the outside if you have any," Mandla added. "That'd help waterproof it even more."

Mr. Thema stood, arms re-folded. "Tar, yeah, I got some. Fine. I'll do that." He stared at the pot a moment longer, then turned his stern gaze on the kids. "I suppose I owe you for this. What's your price?"

Niya stated a sum that matched the effort and materials they used. She kept her voice strong, but Naledi could sense her nerves. The pot was bigger than anything they'd fixed before, after all. Mr. Thema grumbled about young folks charging so much, but eventually he dug into a pouch and counted out coins with a reluctant sigh.

Naledi held her breath, feeling each coin's clink like a note in a half-finished melody. *Please be enough,* she silently begged. When Mr. Thema's hand stilled, Niya scooped the coins into her palm, giving a respectful bow. "Thank you," Niya said.

He gave a curt nod. "If it leaks tomorrow, you'll hear from me." With that, he hoisted the pot back inside, leaving them to gather their tools in the clearing gloom.

Outside, the wind had picked up, kicking dust across the storehouse yard. The sky was a darker gray now, ominous and close. Niya and Mandla exchanged a glance, and Naledi exhaled slowly. "Think we have enough to pay for the flute?" she ventured. She didn't want to sound selfish, but the coins in Niya's hand felt tantalizingly close to the sum needed.

Niya offered a hesitant smile. "We might, but we gotta see how many we already spent on rivets. Let's count properly. Also, remember we're partners ; some of this goes into more materials if folks need more fixes soon."

TIES THAT STRAIN, DREAMS THAT PERSIST

Naledi first felt it in the wind that whipped through the village at midday ; a prickly sort of tension, as though the very air carried a rumor of what lay ahead. The sky was clear enough, but the gusts hissed and kicked up dust in whirlwinds around the Great Tree, sending whispers through its leaves like secret messages. She paused her errands by Malume Nathi's shop, flute tucked under her arm, and wondered why she felt so uneasy.

"Storm coming?" Niya asked, appearing behind her with a small crate of repaired spoons. She'd seen the distant frown on Naledi's face.

Naledi shrugged. "No sign of rain yet. But something feels off." She couldn't name it ; just a stir in her gut that the world had shifted. Perhaps it was only the scattered clouds drifting in, or the hint of dryness in the wind. But in the pit of her stomach, she suspected more than weather.

They soon found Mandla at the edge of the market, fiddling with a broken lantern he planned to fix. He raised an eyebrow at Naledi's distant expression. "You look spooked, Naledi. Something wrong?"

She tried to shake off the feeling. "Not sure. Might be just me. Let's see if we can sell that lantern once you mend it, then maybe we'll ; "

A voice cut through the crowd, carrying an edge of excitement. "They're saying some big men from the city are coming soon ; maybe wanting to buy land." A villager Naledi half-recognized hustled past, arms loaded with sacks of grain. Another woman trailing him murmured, "They'll pay a fortune if they do. Suppose they want to expand the roads or farmland."

Niya glanced at Naledi. "Land? Our village? We barely have enough for ourselves ; why would city folks want it?"

Mandla shrugged, tapping a bent nail straight. "Could be any reason. But folks do say the Great Tree stands on prime ground. You know how outsiders see a big tree and wonder if it'd be better as timber."

Naledi's stomach knotted. *Timber,* she thought. *That can't be.* The Great Tree was more than lumber ; it was the village's silent guardian, her father's memory, the heart of her budding music. If men from the city saw only wood, they could fell it in a day.

A prickling sense of alarm took hold. "We should find out more," she said quietly, glancing around at the bustling market. "I don't like the sound of it."

Niya agreed. "Let's ask around after we close up shop. Maybe Mama Lindiwe knows something."

They kept themselves busy for the next hour, Mandla mending the lantern's handle while Niya haggled with a neighbor over the cost of repaired pots. Naledi kept half her mind on business, half on the vague rumors swirling. The morning sun climbed, shadows shortening, but her worry only deepened.

By midday, Niya ran off to deliver newly fixed utensils, leaving Naledi and Mandla alone. Naledi turned to see Boikonyo standing near Zanele's stall, arms folded, speaking in low tones to a stranger ; a tall man in pressed clothes, a city air about him. Naledi couldn't make out the words, but the man gestured in the direction of the Great Tree, wearing an assessing frown. Boikonyo nodded once, his face grim.

Naledi's breath caught. *What is he discussing?*

When the man moved on, Naledi slipped closer, flute under her arm, Mandla following. Boikonyo noticed them, scowled faintly, then sighed. "No use hiding it," he said, voice taut. "That fellow's from the city. Came to see if our land might be for sale, especially the patch where the big tree stands."

Mandla stiffened. "For what purpose?"

Boikonyo glowered. "Might be a road, might be farmland, might be a new building. All I heard is talk of a wealthy investor wanting to expand. They'd pay a sum for the land ; maybe help us modernize." He let out a frustrated hiss. "He asked me how the village might feel if the tree was taken down. I told him we'd need a meeting."

Naledi's heart hammered, a cold wave rushing through her. "The Great Tree… we can't just cut it," she whispered, hugging the flute closer. "It's part of our home."

Boikonyo lifted a shoulder in a resigned shrug. "Times change, Naledi. Some folks might welcome the money. Or say the tree's in the way." He paused, voice softening. "I know it matters to you, but we can't ignore practical benefits. We've a leaky roof, old huts, half a fence ; money solves a lot."

She stared at him in disbelief. "At what cost?" Her voice shook with the force of her feelings. "It's not just a tree ; it's our root, our anchor, my father's memory." *And my music,* she thought, tears threatening.

Boikonyo's gaze flickered with conflict. "We'll see, Naledi. This is bigger than just us."

She clenched her jaw, turning away to avoid letting tears fall. Mandla laid a supportive hand on her shoulder, his own eyes troubled. Boikonyo pursed his lips, stepping back. "Better hear it from the elder or the headman soon," he muttered, then strode off, the tension in his posture plain.

Naledi swallowed hard, hearing echoes of father's half-played tune reverberating in her mind. *If they level the land, they'll tear down the tree. My flute… father's dream… everything lost?*

Mandla gave her shoulder a small squeeze. "We'll figure it out, Naledi. Don't let Boikonyo's words overshadow your hope."

She nodded, breath shaky. "Let's find Niya. And Mama Lindiwe, too. We need to know if this is real or just talk."

They tracked down Niya near the scrap stall, finishing a sale of refurbished spoons. Quickly, Mandla relayed Boikonyo's news. Niya's eyes widened. "Buy the land for a road or farmland? The Great Tree stands right in the middle of that prime patch, doesn't it?"

Naledi's pulse pounded. "That's what they might want. Think how easy it'd be for them to say, 'Cut the tree, flatten the ground, build something new…'" She broke off, tears biting at the corners of her eyes.

Niya's face hardened. "We can't let that happen. The tree's our village anchor, and your father's memory, too. We should talk to Mama Lindiwe or Malume Nathi. They might've dealt with outside threats before."

Mandla nodded, setting aside a small box of nails. "Let's go now. If a storm's coming, best be prepared."

They hurried through the midday heat, the dusty paths shimmering under the sun. People scurried about, busy with chores or talk of the rumored land sale. Whispers rose at every corner ; some excited about potential compensation, others uneasy about losing the village's identity. Naledi heard one man exclaim, "If they pay me enough, I'll move," while another shouted, "We can't sell our souls for a few coins!" Each passing voice fanned Naledi's dread.

They found Mama Lindiwe sitting on her usual stool under a small awning, weaving a basket from dried reeds. She eyed them knowingly as they approached, cane resting by her side. "I see worry in your eyes," she croaked, motioning them to come closer. "Word travels fast. The outside world wants to buy our land, mm?"

Naledi nodded, throat tight. "Yes, Mama Lindiwe. They might cut the Great Tree. We can't let that happen."

Mama Lindiwe sighed, setting aside her basket. "I feared such a day might come. That tree's older than our grandfathers' grandfathers. It sheltered us from storms, gave travelers shade. Some say its roots hold the village's stories, tied up in memory."

Mandla crouched near her. "Is there a way to protect it? Legally, or through the council?"

Niya added, "We can't pay enough to stop them. Our scrap shop doesn't earn that much."

Mama Lindiwe pursed her lips, gaze distant. "A challenge, indeed. But sometimes hearts unite over what's precious. If enough of the village refuses, who can force them? Unless they have the law on their side…" Her voice trailed off, a deep sadness weighing it down.

Naledi gripped her flute, tears brimming. "My father's memory is in that tree. My music is in it, too. If they cut it, I'll lose my anchor." She swallowed, imagining a bare patch of earth in place of the towering branches. The thought crushed her spirit.

Mama Lindiwe reached out, patting Naledi's trembling hand.

"Child, storms blow in from nowhere. But remember: we've weathered them before. If we stand together, maybe this one, too, shall pass." She glanced at the flute. "Keep playing. Sometimes the right song sways hearts more than any argument."

Niya nodded firmly. Mandla's jaw set with resolve. Naledi inhaled, though her chest felt hollow. "We'll do what we can. Thank you, Mama Lindiwe."

By late afternoon, the once-bright sky dulled with a strange haze. Dust gusted in quick bursts, stinging Naledi's eyes. She found a quiet moment to slip away, her thoughts churning. She needed the Great Tree's calm ; if only for a moment. Arriving at the familiar trunk, she pressed her palm to the bark. *They threaten to cut you down,* she thought, tears pricking. *What am I without you?*

She took a shaky breath and lifted her battered flute to her lips. The first few notes quivered, revealing her turmoil. Memories of father's half-formed tune crashed in, the sense of hope it had given her now overshadowed by the possibility of losing everything. Her breath hitched, producing a sour squeak. She lowered the flute, trembling. *I can't even play right now. My heart's too heavy.*

A nearby voice made her jump. "Naledi?"

She turned to see Malume Nathi, the wise shopkeeper who'd first sold them scraps. He stood quietly, cane in hand, concern in his eyes. "I see the storms in your soul, child," he said gently, stepping forward. "I've heard the rumors, too. The Great Tree is in danger."

Naledi just nodded, tears slipping down her cheeks. Malume Nathi sighed, resting a hand on the trunk. "This tree has stood longer than any of us. But outsiders see only land value, not spirit. If the village stands divided, the city men will take advantage."

She forced her voice steady. "What can we do? Some want the money... we can't force them to keep the tree if they see no worth in it."

Malume Nathi's gaze lingered on the flute in her hand. "They see no worth in intangible things, but intangible things can hold immense power. You can't buy a memory or a melody with coin. You can't weigh tradition and say it's worthless just because it doesn't fill your pocket. Perhaps your music ; your father's dream ; can remind them."

A spark lit in Naledi's chest. *Music as persuasion,* she thought. She pictured the village gathered, hearing the tune she'd cobbled from father's lines. Could it sway enough hearts to stand firm? Or would the promise of modern roads and compensation drown out her quiet flute?

Still, she recalled Mama Lindiwe's words: *Music can unify.* She wiped her tears, clinging to hope like a lifeline. "I'll try," she whispered. "I'll keep playing, and we'll warn folks about what we stand to lose."

Malume Nathi nodded, setting a comforting hand on her shoulder. "We'll gather soon, you'll see. And in storms, be they real or figurative, we discover who we truly are."

Naledi watched him fade back into the dusty paths, leaving her alone with the looming branches overhead. She took another breath, placed the flute to her lips again. Despite her shaking hands, she forced a simple line of melody ; father's gentle opening notes. This time, the sound flowed clearer, sorrow-tinged but resolute. *Yes,* she thought, letting the last note hang. *A storm is coming. We might lose the tree... or we might find a way to save it.*

The sun dipped lower, the wind rattling leaves as though echoing her resolution. She turned away, heart still pounding. *I must gather allies,* she thought. *If the Great Tree falls, a piece of me falls with it. Father's memory, my music... it's all tied together.*

That night, she lay awake on her mat, the wind howling faintly outside like a herald of news not yet told. She clutched the flute to her chest, pondering how storms come in many forms: Some blow in fierce with thunder and rain, while others creep in quietly, cloaked in the promise of progress and coin. *Which is more destructive?* she wondered. *The raging tempest, or the subtle erosion of what we hold dear?*

And there, in the hush before sleep claimed her, another question coalesced ; one not just for her, but for all who wrestle with changes that threaten to uproot the precious threads of tradition and personal dreams.

> *When the storm of outside forces howls at our door, do we cling to the old ways as immovable anchors, or risk welcoming the new, hoping we don't lose our very heart in the exchange?*

She let this question swirl in her mind, uncertain if the future lay in compromise or defiance. For the Great Tree, for her music, and for the village's soul, the reckoning drew near. And perhaps, dear readers, *you* too must grapple with such storms in your own life ; so ask yourself:

> *Which keeps us rooted more ; practical gain or the intangible treasures of memory, art, and the quiet voice of a flute?*

WHEN OLD VOICES STIR

The morning sun crept lazily over the horizon, casting long shadows across the village's dust-laden paths. Naledi awoke to the familiar scent of frying maize cakes wafting from the kitchen, a comforting reminder that life in the village moved in predictable rhythms. Yet today felt different. There was an undercurrent of unease, a silent tension that seemed to hang in the air like the lingering scent of rain after a storm.

She slipped out of her mat and padded barefoot to the hut's entrance, careful not to wake Zanele, who was already bustling about, tending to the morning chores. The broken flute, now a symbol of her quiet rebellion and burgeoning dreams, rested on the low shelf by her bedroll. Her fingers brushed its rough surface, a silent promise to herself that she would continue nurturing this fragile connection to her father's legacy.

As Naledi moved towards the kitchen, she heard the unmistakable sound of Boikonyo's voice, sharp and unyielding, cutting through the morning's calm. He stood near the doorway, arms crossed, his stern gaze fixed on her.

"Naledi," he called, his tone brooking no argument. "We need to talk."

She paused, heart skipping a beat. Boikonyo was a man of few words, his discipline and practicality a stark contrast to her own dreamy nature. "What is it, Boikonyo?"

He stepped closer, the light from the kitchen casting his shadow long and foreboding on the wall. "It's about that flute of yours," he said, gesturing towards the broken instrument. "It's been nothing but trouble. You spend too much time with it instead of helping out around here."

Naledi felt a pang of frustration, her dreams colliding with her responsibilities. "I'm not wasting time," she replied quietly. "Music is important to me."

Boikonyo snorted, the sound harsh in the quiet morning. "Important? You've got chores piling up, and you're more interested in tinkering with broken instruments than fixing the roof before the next storm hits. We can't afford to be so careless."

She took a deep breath, trying to keep her voice steady. "I understand that, but the tree needs us too. It's part of our home, our legacy. And music helps me think, helps me find peace."

Boikonyo's jaw tightened, eyes narrowing. "Peace? We need to be practical, Naledi. Practicality ensures our survival. Dreaming won't fix the roof or protect the tree."

Zanele emerged from the kitchen, wiping her hands on her apron. She watched the exchange with a mixture of concern and sadness. "Boikonyo," she began softly, stepping between her daughter and son, "there's room for both practicality and dreams. Naledi's music is part of who she is."

Boikonyo glanced at his mother, frustration evident in his posture. "Mama, you know we need to prioritize. The roof has a leak that needs patching before the next rain, and the fence is barely holding. We can't have things falling apart because she's distracted by that broken flute."

Zanele sighed, her eyes meeting Naledi's with a silent plea for understanding. "Boikonyo, I hear your concerns. But Naledi's dreams are not a distraction ; they're part of what makes her strong. We need to find a balance."

Boikonyo shook his head, the lines of stress deepening on his face. "Balance? How do you balance saving the roof with nurturing a broken flute? We don't have the luxury to indulge in whims when our home is falling apart."

Naledi felt tears prick at the corners of her eyes, but she blinked them back, standing her ground. "The tree is part of our home, too. If it falls, so do we. And music can bring the community together, remind us of what we're fighting to protect."

Boikonyo's expression softened slightly, but his resolve remained unshaken. "Music is fine when everything is in order. But when things aren't, we need to focus on survival. The tree's roots are strong now, but they won't hold forever if we neglect our duties."

Zanele reached out, placing a gentle hand on Boikonyo's arm. "He's not saying it's not important. Just that we need to manage our time wisely. Naledi, you can continue your music, but also help with the repairs. We need both your creativity and your hands."

Boikonyo glanced at his mother, then at Naledi. "Fine," he muttered, though his eyes held a lingering frustration. "But don't expect me to admire your flute as you do."

Naledi nodded, swallowing her hurt. "I don't need your admiration, Boikonyo. I just need your support."

He turned away, the door swinging shut behind him with a finality that left Naledi feeling hollow. Zanele turned back to her, her eyes filled with empathy. "I know it's hard, Naledi. But we have to work together. Your music is a gift, not a burden."

Naledi stepped closer, resting her hand gently on her mother's. "I want to help, Mama. I'm not abandoning my duties. I just need to find a way to balance both."

Zanele smiled softly, squeezing her daughter's hand. "We'll figure it out. Together."

The rest of the morning passed in a blur of small tasks. Naledi helped Zanele measure flour for the day's batch of dough, her fingers occasionally brushing the flute's worn edges as she worked. Boikonyo busied himself with inspecting the roof, finding weak spots that needed immediate attention. The tension from earlier lingered, a silent storm that neither of them fully addressed.

As noon approached, the village prepared for the upcoming market day. Stalls were set up with fresh produce, woven baskets, and handcrafted goods. Naledi found herself torn between her chores and the pull of the Great Tree, its silent majesty calling her to seek solace in its shade.

After lunch, she wandered out into the yard, the sun warm but not oppressive. She heard the distant sound of hammering; Mandla and Boikonyo likely finishing up another fence repair. Instead of joining them, Naledi felt drawn towards the Great Tree, the place where she had always felt a deep connection.

Underneath its vast canopy, she found a quiet corner, the ground soft with brownish-green grass. The tree's massive roots twisted and turned, creating natural seats and hiding spots. She took a deep breath, feeling the hush around her father's memory envelop her. Then, she retrieved her flute from its cloth wrap, fingers tracing the carvings etched into the bamboo.

She played a gentle note, clear and sweet, letting it float on the breeze. Then another, building a simple melody that felt both new and familiar. Her mind wandered to the conversations she'd had with Mama Lindiwe and the half-finished tune that had started to take shape in her heart.

As she played, a faint rustling stirred the leaves above, and Naledi felt a presence, a whisper of something greater. *Is this what my father felt?* she wondered, letting the music guide her fingers and breath. Each note was a step closer to understanding herself and her place in the world.

From behind a nearby root, she heard a soft chuckle. Turning, she saw Boikonyo stepping into the shade, his expression unreadable. He watched her for a moment, then approached slowly.

"Naledi," he began, his voice softer than she had ever heard it before. "I didn't mean to push you away earlier."

She stopped playing, flute still at her side. "It's okay, Boikonyo. I know you're worried about us."

He sighed, scratching the back of his neck. "I just... I don't want anything bad to happen to our home. The tree, the hut, everything we've built together. And sometimes, I don't understand why you spend so much time with that flute."

Naledi stepped closer, meeting his gaze. "Music helps me cope. It connects me to Dad, to the tree, to the village. It's not just about dreaming; it's about feeling and remembering."

Boikonyo looked away, frustration mingling with a hint of curiosity. "Music, huh? I never took you for a musician."

She smiled softly. "Maybe it's something I was meant to be. Like how you're so good at fixing things."

He glanced back at her, a flicker of admiration in his eyes. "Fixing things isn't as easy as it looks. It takes patience and precision. Maybe music is similar in its own way."

Naledi nodded, sensing a shift in his demeanor. "It does require patience. And maybe, like fixing a roof or a fence, it's about building something that lasts."

Boikonyo's stern facade began to soften, revealing the underlying care he held for his sister. "I suppose you're right. Maybe I've been too hard on you. We need you here, but I also see that your flute means something to you."

She reached out, placing a hand on his arm. "Thank you, Boikonyo. I don't want to fight against you or Mama. I just want to find a way for all of us to thrive."

He sighed deeply, the lines of stress on his face easing. "I guess we both want the same thing ; our family, our home, our future. Maybe we can figure out how to support each other better."

Naledi felt a surge of hope. "I'd like that. Maybe we can set aside specific times for chores and for music. That way, neither gets neglected."

Boikonyo considered her suggestion, then nodded slowly. "It's worth a try. I can help with the repairs, and you can work on your music. Just promise me you won't forget your responsibilities."

She smiled, relief washing over her. "I promise. And maybe your practicality can help me structure my music better."

He chuckled, a sound that seemed foreign yet familiar. "We make a good team, don't we?"

They stood together, the tension of the morning dissipating as they found common ground. Zanele emerged from the kitchen, having finished her own tasks, and joined them under the Great Tree's shade.

"I saw you two talking," she said, her voice warm and understanding. "I think this is a good step. We can all support each other in our own ways."

Boikonyo nodded in agreement. "Thanks, Mama. I think we needed this talk."

Naledi felt a sense of unity she hadn't felt in a long time. "We're stronger together," she said softly, looking from her mother to her brother. "Both in our work and our dreams."

Zanele smiled, her eyes reflecting the resilience that had carried them through so many hardships. "Indeed. And who knows? Maybe your music can inspire more to protect the tree and our way of life."

Naledi's heart lifted at her mother's words. "That's what I hope for. Music can bring people together, remind them of what we're fighting to preserve."

Boikonyo looked thoughtfully at the Great Tree, then back at Naledi. "I'll support your music, Naledi. As long as you help us keep our home safe, we can make this work."

She nodded gratefully. "Thank you, Boikonyo. I appreciate it."

They spent the rest of the morning working together, repairing the roof and reinforcing the fence with renewed teamwork. The harmony between them felt like the beginning of a new melody ; one where each note complemented the other, creating a stronger, more resilient chord.

As the sun climbed higher, the village buzzed with the preparations for market day. Naledi found herself balancing her duties with small breaks to practice her flute, the melodies blending with the sounds of daily life. Niya and Mandla worked diligently at their scrap shop, transforming discarded items into valuable goods, embodying the village's spirit of resilience and creativity.

In the quiet moments under the Great Tree, Naledi's connection to music deepened. She began to experiment with new tunes, inspired by her father's scribbles and her brother's practical wisdom. Her music became a bridge between the old and the new, between dreams and reality, and between her and her family.

One evening, as the village settled into the soft embrace of twilight, Naledi sat under the Great Tree, her flute in hand. Boikonyo approached, a repaired tool bag slung over his shoulder, his expression thoughtful.

"You know," he began, taking a seat beside her, "I was thinking about what you said earlier. Maybe your music can help us in ways I hadn't considered. Like bringing the community together, or even calming the goats when they get too rambunctious."

Naledi laughed softly, the sound mingling with the evening breeze. "I'd like that. If my music can help, I'm all for it."

Boikonyo nodded, his eyes reflecting a newfound respect. "I think I see now how your flute isn't just an instrument ; it's a part of our family's story, too. Maybe we can incorporate it into our daily lives more."

As they sat together, the melodies flowing from Naledi's flute echoed the harmony they were striving to achieve within their family. The Great Tree stood tall and silent above them, a symbol of endurance and growth, much like the bonds they were rebuilding.

And with that thought, she let the night embrace her, the echoes of her music and her family's newfound unity blending seamlessly into the village's enduring rhythm.

Naledi felt a sense of peace settle over her. The conflicts and tensions that had once seemed insurmountable were now avenues for deeper understanding and connection. Her music was no longer just a personal escape but a communal thread weaving their stories together.

Later that night, as the village lay cloaked in the soft darkness of stars, Naledi reflected on the day's events. She realized that her journey with music was not just about personal discovery but about honoring her father's legacy and strengthening her community's resilience. The broken flute, once a source of contention, had become a beacon of hope and unity.

In the quiet solitude of her hut, Naledi picked up her flute, playing a soft, lingering note. It resonated through the walls, a gentle reminder of the harmony they had found amidst tension. As the sound faded into the night, she pondered a question that had been lingering in her heart:

> *Isn't it strange how the melodies we create can shape the very fabric of our lives, binding us to our past and guiding us into the future?.*

WHEN OLD VOICES STIR

Evening crept upon the village with the slow grace of a cat prowling just before moonrise;soft, measured, and full of promise. The sky glowed a dusky red and purple, as though the sun itself couldn't bear to leave, and the air was ripe with the mingled scents of simmering stews, freshly turned earth, and the faint hint of cooking-fire smoke. It was the kind of evening that made a body want to linger outdoors, savoring the hush that settles when daily tasks are done and folks finally have a moment to breathe.

Naledi was seated cross-legged beneath the Great Tree, its broad, ancient boughs arching overhead like protective arms. The village had gathered in that very spot more times than anyone could count, but tonight felt different. Whispers had spread all day that Mama Lindiwe;oldest in the village and keeper of its deepest lore;would be spinning one of her tales. And when Mama Lindiwe decided to speak, even the surliest goat-herder would pause to listen.

"Naledi!" came a bright call. Niya bounded up the path, Mandla following behind in a quieter stride. "Mama Lindiwe's on her way, and she's bringing her old drum along!"

Naledi perked up at once, giving her dust-streaked skirt a hasty brush. "Her drum?" she echoed, trying to keep the excitement from skipping out of her voice. "But she hasn't touched that in years."

Mandla gave a shrug, a small smile hovering at the corner of his mouth. "She claims it only speaks when the story calls for it."

Meanwhile, villagers trickled in from every corner, forming a loose ring around the base of the tree. Children plunked themselves down in front, legs folded, staring wide-eyed at the clearing with that electric sort of anticipation only children can produce. The grown-ups settled where they could;some perched on gnarled roots, others on stools or worn blankets. Zanele arrived with a woven basket draped over one arm, her face expectant yet calm. Even Boikonyo ambled over from a long day of repairing fences, his posture guarded, arms folded as if to say, *I'm here, but I'm not sure I approve.*

At last, Mama Lindiwe emerged from the dusk, tap-tapping her way across the packed earth with her walking stick. A hush fell over the gathering like a cloak. The old drum nestled under her arm looked worn enough to have seen a century of stories, its leather shining and taut. Her silver hair caught the last glimmer of daylight, giving her a certain glow;like a bridge between the past and the present.

"Good evening, children," she said, her voice a warm rasp, like embers stirring in a hearth. "You've all come, and the Great Tree welcomes you." She sat on a low stool right at the base of the trunk, then patted the drum as though greeting an old friend. "Listen close now. The tree will do some of the talking, but I'll lend it my voice."

An expectant hush fell, and Mama Lindiwe began her tale.

"Long, long ago," she said, "before these huts stood here;when the land was bare, and folk scraped by with more hope than harvest;the sky refused us water. Drought baked the fields, and not a drop of rain graced our parched throats. People prayed, but the heavens seemed to hold tight to every cloud. They turned at last to a mere sapling, no taller than you or me, that grew right where this mighty trunk stands now. 'You have roots,' they told it, 'roots that reach deeper than we can see. Help us find the water we cannot.'"

At that, she gave the drum a gentle thump: a single, resonant heartbeat echoing across the clearing. All eyes were on her, children straining to catch each syllable. Naledi felt her own heart pick up a beat, and the hair on her arms stood on end. She thought of her father's half-finished melody, how music might hold answers for what words leave unsaid.

Mama Lindiwe continued, her voice dipping low: "And so the villagers sang to the sapling. Not with fancy instruments or big words;no, they sang with what they had: sorrow, faith, determination. Their voices rose at dawn and at dusk, calling on the tree's roots to find the hidden streams beneath the dusty ground. And do you know, children? That little sapling listened."

The drumbeat deepened, speeding up like raindrops beginning to fall. "Next morning, a thin trickle of water bubbled near its base;cool, clear, and sweet. The drought didn't vanish, but the people endured. They kept singing until the rains found their way home again."

She paused, letting the crowd absorb the wonder of that small miracle. Naledi saw the silhouettes of neighbors leaning forward, caught up in a story that felt both ancient and immediate. The Great Tree's leaves stirred, as though remembering that long-ago moment when it was just a sapling with a song in its roots.

Mama Lindiwe smiled. "That's why we treasure this tree," she said, voice hushed in reverence. "It's not just a tangle of wood and leaves; t's a keeper of our voices. There's power in unity and in music, my children. You raise your voice, and you just might raise another's hope along with it."

Then her gaze fell upon Naledi, and a peculiar warmth lit the old woman's eyes. "And sometimes, music helps us find truths we didn't know we were missing."

A gentle ripple spread through the crowd, the tension within them easing as though some invisible knot had been loosened. The children exhaled in unison, returning to their quiet fidgeting. Adults exchanged smiles or thoughtful nods. Boikonyo remained near the back, his shoulders less rigid than before.

When the tale ended, the villagers lingered under the tree's canopy. Children, set free from the hush, scampered around the roots, giggling. Elders chatted in low voices about the days before, of other times Mama Lindiwe had beaten her drum to carry a story. Naledi sat with her flute on her lap, each breath she took feeling more precious than usual.

"It's beautiful," she murmured, half to herself. Niya and Mandla appeared at her side, plunking themselves down in the soft dirt.

"You're thinking about your father's tune again, aren't you?" Niya asked, her voice gentle as a breeze.

Naledi nodded, fiddling with the flute's carved edges. "Yes. Mama Lindiwe's story reminded me that songs can be more than just notes. They can be… a bridge, or a well, or something bigger than we can explain."

Mandla leaned back against the tree, his eyes half-closed in contemplation. "Maybe that's how we rally folks against those surveyors. We can talk and protest all we like, but nothing moves a heart like a good song."

Niya grinned, tapping a small rhythm on her knees. "A protest circle with music. Think the older ones might join in?"

A faint laugh escaped Naledi. "If Mama Lindiwe can bring out her drum, anything's possible. Though we'd need a reason strong enough to pull everyone together."

Just then, a shadow fell across them. Boikonyo stood there, hands shoved into his pockets, trying (and failing) to mask a hint of curiosity. "Still daydreaming, I see."

Naledi matched his gaze, noticing that his posture wasn't as combative as usual. "Not daydreaming," she said simply. "Just... thinking about how to protect the tree."

He grunted, glancing at the ancient trunk behind them. "Then keep thinking. The talk of outside buyers is stirring again. We might see them soon."

The hush that fell on the trio wasn't as sharp as fear, but it had the edge of worry. Boikonyo turned away, pacing a few steps. Then he paused. "That story," he added, nodding toward Mama Lindiwe, "it's a reminder that sometimes folks do the impossible when they're pushed to a corner." His tone softened, so quiet Naledi almost missed it. "Father believed in that too, you know. He always said a song could move a mountain."

Mandla raised an eyebrow, but kept his silence. Niya's grin widened a fraction. Naledi felt her chest twist in something like hope. "Then maybe we can move this mountain too," she said. Boikonyo didn't reply; just gave a curt nod and walked off, his shoulders carrying an unnamed burden.

Night settled in, each star flickering awake in the velvety sky overhead. The villagers slowly dispersed, returning to their huts with the story's message humming in their ears. Naledi lingered, letting the last remnants of conversation drift away until only a handful of neighbors remained, banked fires glinting faintly in the distance.

Mama Lindiwe approached once more, her drum now quiet at her side. "You see, child," she said, her voice hardly louder than the night breeze, "stories ain't just old words. They're seeds, and they sprout where they're needed."

Naledi nodded, wrapping her arms around the flute. "Do you think we can truly protect the tree from outsiders who have the money and the power?"

Mama Lindiwe's eyes gleamed, ancient and playful all at once. "We protected it before, in storms and droughts. Sometimes we offered words, sometimes we offered song. I reckon if we stand together again, it might do the trick."

Naledi's heart fluttered. She rose to her feet, exhaustion settling in, but beneath it lay a renewed determination. "Thank you for telling the story tonight," she said softly.

Mama Lindiwe chuckled. "I merely passed it along. The tree's the one that's kept it safe all these years."

With that, the old woman tapped her stick and wandered off. Naledi stood alone for a moment, the Great Tree's shadow a comforting cloak. In the stillness, she raised the flute to her lips and played a single, soft note;just enough to echo the memory of her father's half-finished tune. And if the leaves rustled in response, or if the night air carried the faintest whisper back to her, she didn't doubt it for a moment.

Back at home, the hut was warm and dimly lit by a small lantern. Zanele dozed on her mat, a thin blanket over her shoulders. Naledi set her flute aside, careful not to wake her mother. She lay down, the sounds of the day swirling in her mind: Mama Lindiwe's drumbeats, the hush of the crowd, Boikonyo's quiet admission about their father. And in the midst of it all, that question:

> *When the time comes, can music truly unite the village;enough to save the Great Tree, enough to save our home?*

She wasn't sure of the answer, but her heart felt lighter than it had in weeks. Perhaps Mama Lindiwe was right: a story is a seed, and a song is the root that binds it to the earth. Tomorrow, perhaps, that seed would sprout a plan, one that carried in its leaves the hopes of everyone who called this place home.

And with that final, comforting thought, Naledi drifted into sleep, a soft, unspoken melody playing at the edge of her dreams;a tune of rain-finding saplings and a village learning to lift its voice again.

MENDINGS AND MURMURS

By all accounts, it was the sort of morning that tiptoes across the land rather than marching in with fanfare. The sun crept up behind the hills, soft and golden, as if it had nowhere special to be and no reason to hurry. Naledi sat cross-legged outside her family's humble hut, absently tracing the weathered seams of her broken flute. She'd taken to calling it "broken," though in truth she felt there was something more restful than ruined in its silence; like it was just waiting for the right touch to awaken.

She breathed in the crisp air. The day promised mild warmth, steady breezes, and none of the old tension that sometimes rattled the village. But Naledi, for all her outward calm, had a swirl of questions drifting through her mind. *Was this flute fixable? Would it ever sing the way she imagined?* Her father's half-remembered tunes teased at her thoughts, echoing faintly like a distant memory you can't quite catch hold of.

A teasing voice broke her reverie. "Talking to that thing again, I see," said Niya, coming up the path in a cheerful skip. A small sack of tools swung from her shoulder, clanking with each bounce.

Naledi looked up, grinning in spite of herself. "I like to imagine it hums back," she answered, hugging the flute to her chest. "Could be all in my head, but you never know."

"Oh, I believe you," Niya teased, dropping onto the ground beside her. "You're already half a musician, if you're hearing voices in a chunk of wood." She laughed, a bright, unguarded sound that lifted Naledi's spirits. "Come on, Mandla's waiting. Seems he's got another big plan, and it'll fall apart without us."

Naledi raised an eyebrow. "Another big plan? Didn't we just repair half the village's broken spoons?"

Niya's eyes sparkled. "Apparently, Maseko's plow blade is so battered it's more rust than steel. Mandla swears we can fix it good as new and earn ourselves some extra coins in the bargain. Maybe we'll get a couple of eggs out of the deal, too."

Naledi glanced at the flute, a small pang of reluctance tugging at her. "Think Malume Nathi might know anything about instruments?" she asked. "He does fix everything else."

Niya shrugged in that carefree way of hers. "Worth a shot. He's got a knack for turning scraps into treasure. Let's see if your flute can catch his eye."

They found Mandla kneeling outside Malume Nathi's legendary scrap shop, an Aladdin's cave of rusted wonders. Malume Nathi;tall, wiry, and wizened as a desert tree;stood over him, observing as Mandla peered at a dull, bent plow blade. Piles of metal parts leaned precariously nearby, each stack hinting at a story waiting to be told.

Mandla straightened, flashing a grin when he saw Naledi and Niya. "Finally! I was starting to worry your flute had sprouted legs and run off."

Naledi rolled her eyes, giving him a playful shove with her foot. "Har-har. I'm here, and so's my flute. You just make sure you don't break any more tools."

Mandla looked mock-offended. "I only break them so I can fix them better." He turned back to the blade, but his smile gave away the joke.

Malume Nathi cleared his throat softly, bringing their banter to a halt. There was a quiet amusement in his eyes, as though he enjoyed watching these youngsters spark off each other. "So, this is the plow that's seen better days," he drawled, resting a hand on its bent edge. "We can try some hammer work, a bit of welding if the metal's not too far gone. Let's see about that."

The trio followed him into the dim interior of his shop. Candles flickered here and there, casting dancing shadows against shelves heaped with an odd assortment of gears, rods, and contraptions that might once have been part of wagons, pumps, or something stranger. The air smelled of oil and rust, with a faint sweet note of sawdust.

As Mandla explained his plan for reshaping the plow blade, Naledi lingered by the door, flute held tight to her chest. Her stomach fluttered, half with nerves, half with hope. Finally, she mustered her courage. "Malume?" she asked, voice softer than she intended.

He paused, turning to meet her gaze. "Yes, child?"

She stretched out her hands, offering the flute. "Niya bought this for me from your shop a while back. It's old and… well, broken, I think. I've tried playing it, but it mostly squeaks or rasps. Do you know if it's fixable? Could it ever sound the way it's meant to?"

Silence hung in the air a moment as Malume Nathi took the flute from her, studying it with keen eyes. He turned it over, traced the cracks near the mouthpiece, ran a thumb along the chipped edges. Then he nodded slowly, as though this battered instrument had just told him a secret. "It's worth the effort," he said at length, voice low. "You can see it was well-made once; someone put their heart into carving these holes. But time and neglect have taken a toll. Repairing it ain't out of the question, but it requires patience and a willingness to learn." He looked up, meeting Naledi's gaze. "Are you ready for that?"

Naledi swallowed, a strange thrill coursing through her. "I; think so."

A faint smile curved Nathi's lips. "Then come over to that workbench. There's resin and small files you'll need. You'll do the patching yourself. You fix it with your own hands, you'll understand it better when it finally sings."

While Mandla hammered away at the plow blade in the adjacent corner;occasionally calling Niya over to hold or position something;Naledi bent over a small bench lit by a single oil lamp. Malume Nathi showed her how to sand the warped wood gently, smoothing it without wearing it too thin. Next came the resin, which she used to seal tiny cracks that threatened to distort any note she might try to play.

Her hands shook at first; this was more delicate work than patching a tin spoon. But with each careful stroke, Naledi felt a curious calm settle in her chest. She recalled her father's half-forgotten tunes, the lingering sense that music was more than just noise. *This flute was meant to make a sound,* she thought, *and maybe I was meant to help it do so.*

By midday, Naledi had repaired the mouthpiece and aligned the holes as best she could, guided by Malume Nathi's patient nods and corrections. A faint film of sawdust clung to her fingertips, but she hardly noticed. The flute looked less pitiful now, more like something that wanted to live again.

Nathi stepped back, crossing his arms. "All right, child," he said, his tone both gentle and expectant. "See if it'll speak."

Naledi's heart thumped as she raised the flute, pressing it carefully to her lips. She inhaled, then blew a soft, steady breath. A single note emerged, wavery but recognizable;a trembling voice, like a newborn lamb finding its legs.

She pulled the flute away, eyes alight with wonder. "It… it made a sound!"

A wide grin broke across Mandla's face, and Niya clapped her hands. Even Malume Nathi's reserve gave way to a hint of satisfaction. "There you go," he said. "She ain't perfect yet, but you've awakened something."

That evening, Naledi found herself under the Great Tree once more, the sky a tapestry of oranges and purples as the sun dipped behind the huts. Niya and Mandla sprawled on the ground nearby, raving about the day's success with Maseko's plow;apparently it cut cleaner than a fabled scythe now. But Naledi's mind was on the flute.

She raised it, inhaling a breath that caught the scent of dusk on the breeze, and played that single note again. This time, she added a tentative second one, then a third, shaping a fraction of a tune that sounded not half-bad. Niya whooped softly, and Mandla shot Naledi an approving thumbs-up.

"Imagine what you'll do in another week," Mandla said.

Naledi lowered the flute, her cheeks glowing. "I just… I never thought I'd be able to fix it."

"That's the trick of a lot of things," Niya said. "You never know until you try."

They lapsed into a comfortable quiet, listening to the tree's leaves rustling overhead. Naledi gazed at the flute, still showing signs of wear and minor fractures. It would need more attention in the days to come;a gentler sanding, perhaps, or an even thinner resin in some places. But its heart was intact, and it had begun to speak.

All around, the village settled into the hush of twilight. Lanterns flickered, and the low drone of conversation drifted from open doorways. A child's laugh rang out across the way, answered by a mother's gentle scolding. It was the hum of daily life;quiet, steady, and real.

Naledi ran her thumb along the instrument's worn groove, thinking of how far they had come: the trio's small scrap enterprise, the hidden wonders of Malume Nathi's shop, the swirling questions about her father's half-finished melodies. This flute, once broken and silent, was now inching toward wholeness. *Isn't that what all of us are doing?* she wondered. *Mending what's broken, finding our voices along the way?*

The thought brought a soft smile to her face. She glanced at Niya and Mandla, their eyes sleepy but content. Tomorrow would bring more chores, more repairs, maybe more arguments with Boikonyo or mysteries about the Great Tree's fate. But for this moment, under the gathering stars, it felt enough that her flute could offer a note or two. Proof that broken things, tended with care, could learn to sing again.

Naledi lifted the flute once more, letting a gentle breeze carry the faint tune. And as it drifted into the hush of the village night, she couldn't help but wonder:

> *How many of us carry something broken inside;something that just needs a little time, a little patience, to discover its true voice?*

FOOTPRINTS BEYOND THE HORIZON

Morning arrived with a quiet sort of determination; a gentle warming of the sky and a slow sweep of golden light across the village. Naledi sat cross-legged beneath the Great Tree, letting the early breeze toy with her hair. Her flute lay across her lap, still showing the signs of careful mending. She'd spent many dawns just like this, pondering how the older notes from her father's half-finished tune seemed to linger in the tree's rustling leaves. Yet on this particular morning, she felt the tug of possibility.

"Naledi!" came a familiar call from the nearby path. Niya bounded up, her cheeks flushed and a swirl of dust dancing at her heels. A little ways behind her, Mandla ambled along in his steady way, a bag of tools rattling against his hip.

"You sure are in a hurry," Naledi remarked, pushing herself to her feet and tucking the flute under one arm.

"We've got news," Niya replied, still catching her breath. "A traveling festival is setting up near the next town; lots of musicians, performers, all kinds of wonders."

Naledi's pulse quickened. She clutched the flute a bit tighter. "Musicians?" she echoed, unable to hide the hope in her voice.

Niya nodded enthusiastically. "So I've heard. Drums, flutes, probably instruments we've never seen. Mama Lindiwe claims it's the biggest event this side of the hills." She shot Mandla a sideways grin. "Might be a rare chance for us to learn a thing or two."

Mandla hefted his tool bag higher on his shoulder. "Heard they've got a market too;a big one. We could pick up parts for the scrap shop if they aren't charging an arm and a leg." He paused, glancing at Naledi. "And maybe someone there knows a thing or two about flutes;could help you polish up your father's melody."

Naledi felt her heart thunder with a mix of excitement and nerves. This might be the chance she'd been longing for;a chance to make sense of the half-finished tune her father left behind. Yet the festival was a fair distance away. The three of them had never gone off so far on their own.

Niya must have read Naledi's thoughts, for she patted her friend's arm reassuringly. "We'll handle the distance if we plan right. Leave early, be back before sundown, or Mama and the rest will drag us home by the ears."

Naledi exhaled, nodding. "All right," she said, feeling a tremor of resolve. "Let's ask for permission and see what happens."

That evening, with the day's chores behind her, Naledi found herself by the cooking fire beside Zanele. The soft crackle of burning wood mingled with the faint scents of fried dough and simmering stew. Zanele's hands were busy shaping tomorrow's maize cakes, but Naledi had her mother's ear for the moment.

"Mama," Naledi began, choosing her words carefully, "Niya and Mandla heard about a festival in the next town. They've got musicians and a big market;maybe even someone who knows how to repair or play flutes. Could we… go see it?"

Zanele paused, dusting flour from her palms. "It's not a quick journey," she said slowly. "Any festival worth its salt tends to draw big crowds;and all sorts of trouble can hide in crowds. Have you thought of that?"

"I have," Naledi admitted. "But Niya and Mandla will be with me. We'd stick together. Mandla never goes anywhere without his tools. He'll chase off trouble with a wrench if he has to."

Zanele's lips twitched, as though suppressing a reluctant smile. "Tools won't fix a broken leg or fend off a clever thief. But…" She let out a soft sigh. "You've been responsible these last few weeks, Naledi;helping in the scrap shop, practicing music, tending chores. If Niya's and Mandla's folks agree, and you promise to be back before dark, I suppose I won't stand in your way."

Naledi's face lit with gratitude. "Thank you, Mama; promise we'll be careful." She hesitated, then added, "And this might be my only chance to really learn about father's tune."

Zanele's gaze softened. "He'd like that, I think. Now hurry up and wash your hands;this dough won't knead itself."

Two days later, the trio set off at dawn. The sun peeked over the hills, bathing the fields in a warm glow that felt both comforting and full of promise. Each carried a small bundle of water and snacks, bracing themselves for the long walk ahead. The trail meandered through gently rolling farmland, where an early breeze carried the scent of wildflowers, freshly turned soil, and the occasional baa of a wandering goat.

Niya led the charge with her ceaseless energy, calling back whenever the path branched. Mandla, ever practical, kept track of the time and pointed out any suspicious rocks or hidden roots that might trip them. Naledi trailed along with her flute nestled safely in a sling across her back, her thoughts swirling with anticipation: *What if we find a real flute expert? Or a traveling musician who knows father's style?* The possibilities drummed a lively beat in her heart.

They passed the last farmstead of their village's territory around mid-morning, waving to a farmer who regarded them with a quizzical smile. "Going far?" he called.

"Just to see a festival," Niya replied, returning a wave.

"Take care, then," he said, tipping his broad-brimmed hat.

As they ventured beyond familiar ground, the trail dipped and rose in gentle slopes. Now and again, they caught the faint notes of distant drums, carried on the wind like an invitation. Naledi's pulse quickened each time she thought she heard a flute in the mix;though it might just have been the breeze.

Finally, by late morning, the festival came into view;a sprawling patchwork of colorful awnings, stalls, and tents set up near the outskirts of the neighboring town. The hum of voices and music reached them first;a joyous, haphazard chorus that made Naledi's skin tingle. On the far side, a handful of wagons and caravans were parked, their exteriors painted with bold images of dancing figures and swirling instruments.

"Look at all those stalls!" Mandla breathed, excitement brightening his face. "And the machines;do you see that contraption?"

Niya followed his gaze. "It's like a giant barrel on wheels. Maybe they cook something in it?"

They stepped into the bustle, eyes wide as their senses flooded with new sights and scents. Vendors hawked fresh-roasted nuts, spiced teas, and sweet pastries topped with all manner of brightly colored syrup. One stall boasted handmade brooms, another displayed vibrant cloth dyed in patterns Naledi had never dreamed possible.

A juggler performed near the center, tossing a flurry of wooden clubs into the air. Beside him, a fire-breather breathed plumes of flame to the delight of a cheering crowd. Niya and Mandla exchanged gleeful looks, marveling at the spectacle, while Naledi clutched her flute, scanning the stalls for any hint of musical instruments.

And then she saw it;a corner stall laden with flutes, drums, stringed instruments, and whistles of every size and shape. An older woman in a flowing shawl stood behind the table, chatting with a customer. Naledi's heart soared; this was exactly what she needed.

They wove through the throng, Mandla pausing only once to inspect a booth displaying strange, gear-laden contraptions. But soon enough, all three stood before the instrument stall. The woman;a kindly face framed by silver hair;greeted them with a smile. "Looking for a tune, are we?"

Naledi nodded, breathless. "I've... I've a flute that was broken. I repaired it a bit, but I want to learn how to truly play. My father left behind a melody, and I can't finish it alone."

The woman's eyes sparkled with interest. "Let me see that flute, child."

With trembling hands, Naledi retrieved the flute from her sling, offering it up. The woman turned it over with practiced care, inspecting the mouthpiece, running her thumb along the holes. "A simple design, but well-crafted," she remarked. "You say you repaired it? Good work;the wood's been smoothed here, the resin sealing looks tidy. And the tuning... well, you might need a proper teacher for that." She beckoned for Naledi to follow. "Come around here. Let's see what sort of tone we can coax out."

Niya and Mandla hovered nearby, exchanging silent, excited glances as Naledi stepped behind the table. The woman plucked a small tuner from a leather pouch;an odd, slender device Naledi had never seen;and blew a single note through it. She listened intently, then had Naledi do the same with her flute. A soft frown crossed the woman's face.

"Your lower register is drifting a bit. May need to tighten the seal," she murmured. Then, with deft fingers, she adjusted one of the lower holes using a minuscule file. She motioned for Naledi to try again.

This time, the tone emerged clear and resonant, filling the corner of the stall with a bright, lilting sound. Naledi's eyes widened in wonder. "It sounds... real," she whispered. "Like a proper flute."

"It is a proper flute," the woman said with a gentle laugh. "You just had to give it the right care." She leaned closer, lowering her voice. "As for that melody your father left, remember: music carries memory. If you follow your heart with it, you'll find the path he started."

Naledi's throat constricted with emotion. She closed her eyes, blew a brief scale, and found the notes rolling out with surprising ease;a modest tune, yes, but full of potential. Niya and Mandla broke into a round of applause, faces alight with pride.

"Thank you," Naledi said, turning back to the woman. "I;how can I repay you?"

The woman waved a dismissive hand. "A few coins for my time, but the rest is goodwill. Seeing a flute reborn is payment enough." She cast a wink at Niya and Mandla. "Though if you have any scraps or oddities to barter, I might take a look."

Mandla brightened instantly, patting his tool bag. "We might indeed. Let me see what I've got."

By midday, they'd secured not only a perfectly tuned flute but also a handful of peculiar odds and ends for their scrap shop;mysterious gears and hinges Mandla believed could be turned to profit. The festival's music, laughter, and bright colors seemed to shine just for them.

They lingered a while longer to watch a traveling musician perform a flute solo near the festival's main stage. Naledi listened in awe as the player danced through rapid trills and soulful descents. She felt her father's tune stirring inside her, eager to find its shape in this newfound realm of possibility.

Eventually, they realized the sun had traveled farther across the sky than intended. With a reluctant sigh, they purchased a final snack;sticky roasted nuts Niya simply couldn't refuse;and made their way back along the winding path toward home. The excitement of the day buzzed between them, their chatter weaving around the memory of the festival's dazzling sights.

"Worth every step, I'd say," Niya declared, popping a sugared nut into her mouth. "Your flute's practically singing on its own now."

Mandla nodded, patting the small satchel of odd metal parts. "And we might have just what we need to upgrade the water pump or fix that generator the neighbors keep complaining about. Imagine the scrap shop's reputation then!"

Naledi, flute tucked securely under her arm, had no regrets about the long hike. Her heart felt light yet determined, like a bird testing newly spread wings. *So many songs yet to learn,* she thought, *and Father's tune is only the beginning.* A renewed sense of confidence filled her;confidence that she could honor the memory of a man who once dreamed too big for village life, and in doing so, perhaps help the whole community dream a little bigger themselves.

As the sun dipped lower, painting the fields with long shadows, the trio entered their village. The sight of the Great Tree rose before them in the final stretch, its branches rustling in greeting. Naledi paused, lifting the flute to her lips. She played a gentle phrase;soft, lingering, just a taste of the melody that danced in her heart. The notes felt smoother than ever, carrying the day's discoveries back home.

Niya and Mandla paused beside her, smiles on their faces. The tune faded into the hush of twilight, its echoes weaving through the leaves. *This is what we came for,* Naledi thought.

A chance to chase rumors and find something real; about music, about hope, about all the broken things we can mend together.

And as they passed under the welcoming shade of the Great Tree, she felt it whisper its ancient encouragement once more: *Keep going, child. Your story has only just begun.*

VOICES FROM FAR-OFF ROADS

The sun rose that morning as though it were a slow-footed traveler, setting out on a journey of its own and kindly inviting the world to follow along. It spread a gentle, honeyed light over the modest village, illuminating each straw hut and meandering path until everything looked as if it had been brushed with gold. Naledi stood at the threshold of this scene with her flute snug in a cloth wrap slung across her shoulder, gazing down a winding road that stretched into territories unknown. Her heart thumped in anticipation, but also in caution, for stepping beyond the village's protective circle of huts was no small matter.

Just behind her, Niya and Mandla finished fussing with their provisions. Niya's bag, bulging in odd shapes, hinted at an odd mix of hammered metal scraps and rations wrapped in cloth. Mandla, who rarely left the village without a tool or two, wrestled with the straps on his pack, ensuring nothing rattled loose.

"You sure we're ready?" Niya asked, pushing a stray braid off her forehead. There was a lively excitement in her voice, tempered by just a pinch of nervousness. "Feels like we ought to double-check everything;like we're forgetting some crucial item."

Mandla offered a reassuring grin. "We have enough food, enough water, and enough coin for whatever the road throws at us. Besides," he added, patting a worn wrench poking from a side pocket, "if trouble finds us, we'll fix it like we do everything else."

Naledi smiled, though her free hand fiddled with the edge of the cloth that sheltered her flute. "I'm about as ready as I'll ever be," she said, turning to her companions. "What do you suppose the town will be like?"

Mandla shrugged his broad shoulders, a playful glint in his eyes. "Bigger, noisier, busier. More smells to sniff, more wonders to see. Maybe they've got a traveling caravan or a festival. Who knows;someone might even hold the key to finishing your father's melody."

Niya nodded. "And let's not forget the real reason we're trekking so far;the water pump we keep trying to upgrade. If we don't come back with that special part, Boikonyo will scold us half to death. And that's if your mother doesn't beat him to it."

They shared a laugh at that;nothing like the threat of familial lectures to keep one's motivation high. With that final note of humor, they stepped away from the outskirts of the village. Behind them, the humble cluster of huts gradually receded, until only the Great Tree stood visible, its lofty branches seeming to wave a gentle farewell. Naledi felt a pang in her chest looking back at it, remembering the nights spent tinkering with her flute under its watchful leaves. But she squared her shoulders. *I'll return with something worth sharing,* she promised silently, taking a breath and forging onward.

The road wound through open grasslands that glimmered in the morning sun like fields spun from threads of gold. Each gentle swell of the ground revealed a new tapestry of wildflowers, bobbing in the breeze as if bowing to the travelers. Occasionally, the trio passed a farmer leading a donkey-laden cart or a small herd of goats shepherded by a watchful child. The villagers they encountered greeted them with polite nods, curious about where such a bright-eyed bunch might be headed.

They hadn't gone far when Niya stopped short, shading her eyes with one hand. "Is that… smoke?" she asked, pointing to a thin plume rising near the horizon. It was hardly more than a wisp, but it caught the sunlight in a way that made it shimmer against the pale sky.

Mandla leaned forward, squinting. "Hard to tell at this distance. Might be from a camp or traveling merchants. Maybe it's the next village's cooking fires warming up for the day."

Naledi pursed her lips, imagining caravans, strange faces, perhaps even an itinerant musician who carried tunes from distant lands. Her father had once talked of such wanderers; how they traveled with instruments slung across their backs, collecting songs as other folk collected coins. The thought spurred her footsteps faster along the path.

The hours passed in a pleasant, lazy fashion, the sun climbing ever higher. At times, the path took them through clusters of thorny brush, at others over gently sloping hills that afforded glimpses of farmland stretching for miles. Birds wheeled overhead, their calls occasionally piercing the calm. Niya pointed out interesting rocks and insect nests, while Mandla couldn't resist pausing now and again to examine a weathered bit of metal or an abandoned wheel hub; "Just in case it's useful," he'd say, earning a half-exasperated, half-amused look from Niya.

Naledi, for her part, held onto her flute like a talisman, letting her mind drift to half-finished melodies. She practiced them silently in her head, picturing how the notes might rise and fall if only she had some guidance from a truly skilled player. *If we meet someone who knows,* she thought, *maybe I'll learn how to fill the empty spaces Father left behind.*

By midday, the grasslands gave way to a hard-packed dirt road, rutted with wheel tracks from carts larger than any they'd seen in their own village. The breeze carried a hint of something new;an aroma of cooking spices, livestock penned up in unseen corrals, and the faint whiff of smoke that Niya had spotted earlier. Each step brought them closer to a place where, so rumor said, a bustling town offered everything from mechanical trinkets to musical wonders.

And sure enough, not long after that, they spied a trio of ramshackle carts parked under a lone acacia tree. Two travelers in dusty clothes were sipping from waterskins, their donkeys tethered to a low branch. At the sight of Naledi and her friends, the travelers lifted their hands in greeting.

"Howdy, youngsters," one called, a wiry fellow with a wide hat. "You off to the market town, I'll wager?"

Niya, ever the outspoken one, answered brightly, "That we are. Is it much farther?"

The fellow shook his head. "Not more than an hour's walk, if your legs are strong. You'll know it by the smell of grilled maize and the noise of haggling folks. Just keep on that track," he said, pointing. "And watch for pickpockets if it's your first time in a big crowd."

They thanked him and moved on, the promise of a thriving market spurring them onward. Naledi's stomach fluttered with anticipation, but also a trickle of nerves. *A big crowd might have pickpockets, but it might also have the musician I need.* She tried to steady her thoughts, inhaling the dusty air that was now tinged with a hint of cooking smoke.

At last, they crested a small rise, and beyond it lay a sight that made Naledi's heart dance: a sprawling market town, bigger than anything she'd seen. Huts and buildings of stone, mud, and timber lined a broad thoroughfare, while rows of stalls fanned out in all directions. A kaleidoscope of colors greeted them;textiles dyed in bright blues and reds, produce stacked in neat pyramids, and banners flapping with the day's breeze. Laughter and haggling voices mixed with the bray of donkeys and the clatter of wheels. And, faintly but unmistakably, came the sound of distant music;drums, maybe a fiddle, and even a flute's high, sweet cry weaving through the din.

Niya's eyes glowed. "This is... more than I pictured," she whispered, standing in awe.

Mandla's grin stretched ear to ear. "Never thought I'd see so many people at once. And look at those machines;are those steam-driven wagons?"

Naledi could only nod, her gaze sweeping the scene. She felt both thrilled and intimidated, the swirl of humanity reminding her how very small their little village was. But she also felt a surge of determination: this was why they came. She reached a hand to pat her wrapped flute, silently promising, *We'll find our help here.*

They entered the main avenue, keeping close to one another for fear of losing themselves among the throng. Vendors shouted from every side;"Fresh bread!" "Hand-carved spoons!" "Spices from across the mountains!";each voice jockeying for attention. A few curious onlookers glanced at the trio, perhaps noticing Niya's homemade bag stuffed with who-knew-what, or Mandla's tool-laden pack, or Naledi's flute wrap. But mostly, folks bustled about their own business, leaving the three travelers to explore.

Mandla spotted a stall full of rusted gears, rods, and mechanical odds and ends that set his heart aflutter. "I'll meet you by that big sign in half an hour," he told the girls. "If we find that water pump part, we're golden."

Niya nodded. "I'll go see if there's a textile vendor who'll swap scraps for leftover wire. Naledi, you want to come along, or;?"

Naledi shook her head, her eyes drifting toward a faint melody drifting from somewhere up the street. "I hear a flute. I think I need to follow that."

Niya shared a quick smile with her, as though to say *Go get your dream*, and hurried after Mandla.

Naledi let her ears guide her along a narrow lane, lined with stalls selling everything from battered boots to colorful hair ribbons. The flute's music grew clearer; trilling high, then dipping low in a graceful arpeggio. She navigated through the crowd until she reached a small clearing between two large buildings. There, perched on a crate, sat a middle-aged woman in a flowing robe, playing a wooden flute that gleamed in the midday sun. A small audience of children and a few curious adults listened, entranced.

Naledi waited at the fringes of the group, flute in hand. The woman's playing was precise yet soulful, each note resonating with a confidence Naledi had only glimpsed in her father's half-remembered hums. When the piece ended, the children clapped and giggled, while the woman offered a modest bow. Then her gaze fell upon Naledi.

"You have a flute there," the flutist observed with a smile. "Care to join me in a duet?"

A wave of heat flushed Naledi's cheeks. "I'm not that good," she mumbled, stepping closer. "But I… I'm trying to learn. My father left a tune unfinished, and I want to complete it. I was hoping someone here might guide me."

The woman's brow rose. "A tune left behind by your father, hmm? That sounds like a calling." She patted the crate beside her, beckoning Naledi to sit. "Show me what you can do."

Feeling as though every eye in the lane was upon her, Naledi settled on the crate, fingers trembling against her instrument. She inhaled, recalling the fragments of the melody that had danced on the edge of her dreams. The first note quivered, but as she played on, her breath steadied. She let the music flow, weaving the notes she remembered with the ones she'd invented to fill the gaps. The flutist watched intently, nodding here and there, her expression serene.

When Naledi finished, the woman gave a thoughtful nod. "There's soul in that tune. Your father's, perhaps, but also yours. It wants a more solid finish, though." She lifted her own flute, demonstrating a few possible endings;one that soared triumphantly, another that resolved in a gentle lull.

Naledi's eyes lit up, absorbing each variation. "That's exactly what I needed to hear. Thank you!" she exclaimed, voice trembling with gratitude.

The flutist chuckled warmly. "Music is a conversation, child, between you and the world. Your father started that conversation;now it's your turn to keep it going. Keep practicing, keep listening, and someday, that tune will become your own."

By late afternoon, Naledi rejoined Niya and Mandla at the prearranged meeting spot, a towering wooden sign proclaiming "Welcome to Addisu Market." Niya had a small bundle of colorful cloth in her arms, having successfully bartered leftover wire, while Mandla carried a dusty mechanical contraption that he swore was the missing piece for their water pump plan. They exchanged tales of their separate adventures, Naledi positively glowing as she recounted meeting the flutist.

"She showed me different endings for Father's tune," Naledi said, excitement charging her words. "And she said the melody's partially mine now. I want to try it under the Great Tree when we get home;see how it sounds there."

Niya squeezed Naledi's shoulder. "I can't wait to hear it. We might have to charge admission if it's as good as you say."

Mandla grinned. "I'll build a stage out of spare boards, and we'll call it the Great Tree Theater."

Naledi laughed, though the idea didn't seem entirely far-fetched. If there was one thing she'd learned, it was that music carried a magic of its own. Perhaps, in time, it might draw the entire village together more powerfully than any argument or petition could.

With the sky softening into dusk hues, they started their trek back home. The road felt less daunting now, as if the day's experiences had stretched their confidence alongside the horizon. They walked in animated conversation, sharing bites of dried fruit Niya had purchased and teasing Mandla about how quickly he'd hopped on the chance to buy old metal parts.

When at last the familiar silhouette of their own village huts emerged, Naledi paused. The Great Tree stood tall and steady, exactly as they'd left it, branches swaying as though in welcome. She touched her flute wrap, heart brimming with gratitude and possibility.

"I think we did well today," Mandla remarked, shifting his pack. "Got the part, found new cloth, and you gleaned your father's tune. Not a bad haul, if I say so myself."

Niya nodded, pushing back a yawn that hinted at her tired feet. "Let's just hope we don't get scolded for coming back on the brink of night."

Their footsteps carried them into the village proper, welcomed by lantern light spilling from windows and doorways. A few neighbors waved, curiosity sparking in their eyes. Naledi imagined how she might soon gather them around, share the newly perfected melody, and let them see that a broken flute;and a half-finished dream;could blossom into something whole.

As the last rays of sunlight disappeared, Naledi cast a final glance at the Great Tree. She could almost sense it whispering encouragement. *Yes,* she thought, lifting her chin, *we journeyed beyond the huts, but we came back with more than we left with. Father's melody grows stronger now, and so do we.*

And in the quiet hush of twilight, she made a silent vow: *One day soon, this tune will echo across the village, a bridge between what was and what can be.*

TRIALS FORGED IN HARMONY

Morning dawned over the village with a clarity so fine you'd have sworn the sun had polished each ray before sending it across the sky. Trees and thatched huts alike stood in crisp outline, the colors of the world suddenly sharper and more alive. Perhaps it was just an ordinary day, but to Naledi;and to Niya and Mandla; t felt like the sort of day where even the world's ordinary corners might yield something extraordinary.

They gathered by the Great Tree, each carrying a small pack of provisions and an abundance of dreams. Niya came first, bright-eyed and practically on tiptoe with excitement. Mandla showed up next, a small parchment list of mechanical odds and ends poking from his pocket, because Mandla seldom traveled anywhere without the comforting knowledge of what spares or tools he might need. Naledi arrived last, flute wrapped carefully in a square of cloth slung across her shoulder, her heart skipping between excitement and apprehension.

"Take a good look," Niya said, patting the tree's trunk as though bidding farewell to an old friend. "It might be a while before we see you again."

The Great Tree, for its part, simply rustled in the gentle breeze, as though giving the trio a silent send-off. They were bound for the bigger market in the next town;a half-day's journey on foot. On the surface, their mission was simple: Mandla needed a rare part to repair the village's water pump, Niya wanted to check on trade goods and bargains, and Naledi hoped;more than anything;to find someone who could mend her father's old flute and perhaps teach her a real tune or two.

"Set, everyone?" asked Mandla, hoisting his bag over his shoulder.

Niya nodded, a sparkle in her eye. "As ready as we'll ever be. Let's not dawdle, or we'll miss all the best deals."

Naledi took one last look at the Great Tree. *I'll be back soon*, she thought, giving it a silent promise. Then she turned, and with that, the three set off, their feet stirring gentle puffs of dust along the road that snaked away from their village and toward unknown territories.

They walked beneath a sky so blue it seemed brand-new, as though the earth and the heavens had agreed it was a day for fresh possibilities. Sunlight bathed the grasslands in warm gold, making each rustling blade seem somehow more alive. The land near their village was flat and friendly, dotted with low shrubs and the occasional acacia tree offering a speck of shade. Hardly a soul stirred at that hour, and the hush of the morning gave their journey a faint sense of secrecy;as if they were sneaking away on some grand undertaking the rest of the world had yet to discover.

"Think they'll have the part?" Niya asked after a quarter hour of mostly cheerful silence. She turned to Mandla, who walked a pace or two ahead. "That water pump is ancient;older than half our huts, by my guess."

Mandla shrugged in that calm, confident way of his. "I wouldn't bet my last coin on it, but if they don't have the exact piece, maybe they'll have something close enough. I can modify or patch it. We'll manage. We always do."

Naledi half-listened, her mind drifting to the flute pressed against her side. She'd barely slept the night before, visions of a traveling musician or wise craftsman dancing through her dreams;someone who would show her the missing pieces of her father's melody. Or, at the very least, help her tune the instrument properly so it would cease its odd squeaks and whispers.

It wasn't long before Niya's teasing voice cut into Naledi's thoughts. "And what about your quest, Flute Girl? We searching for a wizard with a magic wand, or will a half-decent musician do?"

Naledi huffed a laugh, her cheeks warming. "I'll settle for a kind soul who knows a bit about music and can fix a cracked mouthpiece. And if they can teach me a note or two beyond the donkey-like braying I currently manage, that'd be a bonus."

Mandla chuckled, tossing her a reassuring grin. "You do better than a donkey, I promise. Anyway, rumor has it there's a corner in that market known for unusual instruments;Malume Nathi called it the 'lost and found of songs,' or something like that. If anyone can help you put a voice to that flute, it'll be whoever runs that corner."

Naledi breathed a quiet sigh of relief, letting the conversation swirl around her as the road curved onward.

They reached the market by mid-morning. What a sight it was;an explosion of color and clamor all rolled into one bustling scene. Stalls with bright awnings lined both sides of a wide dirt avenue, their canopies flapping in the breeze. Vendors hollered out the merits of their wares: sweet roasted maize, hand-carved stools, woven baskets in every hue. A sea of people flowed through, each stall competing for attention with the next. Goats bleated, dogs barked, and children squealed, weaving underfoot.

"There's more racket here than a startled henhouse," Niya muttered, eyes darting in every direction at once. But she was smiling, obviously thrilled by the chaos.

Mandla surveyed the stalls thoughtfully, fishing out his crumpled list. "We'll get lost if we don't plan. Let's pick a meeting spot."

Niya pointed to a tall, ancient baobab at the market's center, so wide it looked capable of holding half the village in its shade. "How about that tree? Hard to miss."

Satisfied, the trio agreed to reconvene under the baobab in exactly one hour. With that, they dispersed: Mandla, list in hand, marching off to the hardware section, Niya striding after him to haggle prices or bark at dishonest sellers. Naledi watched them go, a ripple of nerves flickering in her belly. Then, hugging her flute wrap close, she plunged into the thick of the market, eyes peeled for any sign of an instrument stall or roving musician.

The crowd jostled her lightly;people from all over, wearing clothes of every style and color, some faces lit with excitement, others creased with bargaining tension. She glimpsed an old man selling sweet dumplings from a steaming pot, a woman hawking dried herbs that filled the air with a pungent tang, and even a fellow stilt-walker ambling through, towering above the throng. Naledi found herself both enchanted and intimidated. This was a far cry from the quiet serenity of her home.

She wandered for a quarter hour without luck, passing stalls loaded with dusty books, mismatched shoes, and exotic fruits she'd never seen. But no flutes or sign of musical repairs. Her hope dimmed slightly. *Could it be just another rumor?*

Then, as she was about to retrace her steps, a gentle piping reached her ears, clear as a birdcall at dawn. She followed the sound, weaving through a tight cluster of onlookers who parted just enough to let her see. There, in a modest corner stall at the market's edge, sat a woman playing a battered lute while a young boy tapped a small drum. A wooden sign above them read "Lost & Found Music." Naledi's heart soared.

She stepped forward, waiting for the tune to end, then cleared her throat softly. The woman looked up, smiling kindly. "Come to listen, have you?"

Naledi offered a shy smile in return. "Yes, and… maybe more than listen." She unwrapped her flute, holding it out. "I; 'm learning to play this. My father left the melody half-finished, but it squeaks a bit. I'm hoping someone could help me fix it… or teach me."

The woman's eyes sparkled with interest. She laid aside the lute, accepted Naledi's flute, and turned it over in her hands. "It's old wood," she remarked, running a fingertip over a faint crack near the mouthpiece. "Some wear around the finger holes, too. That can throw off your sound." She nodded at Naledi. "So, let's see if it's a matter of repairs or technique. Play me a note or two."

Naledi's stomach fluttered, but she lifted the flute to her lips and summoned the little tune she'd coaxed from it before; her father's notes, plus her own attempts at bridging the gaps. The sound emerged halting but recognizable, the flute's voice quivering with a nervous energy that Naledi felt in her very bones.

When she finished, the woman gave a thoughtful hum. "Your approach isn't off, but that crack needs sealing, or you'll never get the proper air pressure. Give me a moment." From a small chest, she extracted a delicate brush, a tiny vial of resin, and a strip of cloth. With gentle precision, she cleaned the flute's damaged area, sealed the crack, and used the cloth to polish and align the mouthpiece. The boy with the drum watched in fascination, eyes wide.

"There," the woman said, handing it back. "Try now, and breathe from your center, not just your throat."

Naledi did as instructed, taking a deeper breath. She let the air flow slowly, focusing on the woman's advice, and a note emerged;clear and steady as a dawn bird's call. Excitement tickled her scalp. She moved her fingers, testing the scale, and each note followed faithfully, no longer rasping or squeaking.

A beaming smile overtook Naledi's face. "I; can't believe it," she whispered. "It's like a whole new flute."

The woman laughed warmly. "An instrument's got a soul of its own, child. You just had to let it speak." She reached over, repositioning Naledi's left hand slightly. "Now, keep practicing, but slow your transitions. If you rush, you'll trip the notes."

Naledi nodded, feeling that rush of gratitude she'd scarcely known she needed. "Thank you," she said, voice thick with emotion. "I can't wait to show my friends, to play for my mother and;" She paused, swallowing. "Maybe honor my father's memory, too."

The woman's eyes flickered with understanding. "Music can unite, soothe, or spark a fire in folks. Keep playing, and who knows what wonders'll follow."

With her flute freshly mended and her spirit brimming, Naledi thanked the woman again, bowed to the boy with the drum, and wove her way back into the market fray. She felt as if she were floating;the entire bustling crowd, with its swirl of sounds and scents, barely registered. All she knew was that the flute at her side no longer felt heavy with doubt. It felt alive;capable of singing her father's tune and maybe a hundred more.

When the hour was nearly up, Naledi made her way to the towering baobab. She found Niya already waiting, devouring a small bag of roasted peanuts with cheerful gusto. Moments later, Mandla arrived, clutching a modest paper package under one arm and wearing a look of deep satisfaction.

"Part secured," he announced triumphantly, nodding at the

package. "Managed to haggle it down, too. With any luck, I'll have the water pump chugging like new by next week."

Niya grinned, fishing out a few peanuts for Naledi. "So? Did you fix that flute, or did you find an ancient wizard to conjure your father's ghost?"

Naledi giggled, cheeks flushing at Niya's dramatics. "No ghosts, but I found a kind woman who repaired the crack and showed me how to hold it properly. Listen!" Without waiting for further coaxing, she lifted the flute and played a simple sequence of notes. No squeaks, no half-rasps;just a clear, humming sound that rose like a promise in the late-morning air.

Niya's eyes went round as melons. "That's miles better than before!"

Mandla clapped Naledi on the shoulder. "You'll be a regular minstrel in no time. Maybe even stir up a crowd if you keep at it."

Naledi lowered the flute, heart pulsing with a heady mix of pride and relief. "I still have to practice, but it feels right now, like the flute is speaking with me, not against me."

With their new treasures and mended instruments, the trio decided to head home before midday heat made travel unpleasant. The road back felt gentler in some way, or perhaps it was just that their burdens were lighter. Niya teased Mandla about showing off the pump part to impress the neighbors, while Mandla teased Naledi about writing entire symphonies. Naledi laughed it off, but inside she nurtured the spark of an idea: *What if I do create something new;something father never had the chance to finish?*

By late afternoon, the village's humble huts emerged in the distance, their thatched roofs lit by the lowering sun. The Great Tree stood sentinel at the outskirts, its broad canopy swaying in a mild breeze as though waving them home. Naledi felt a pang of gratitude for the quiet steadiness of that ancient tree, always ready to greet them as they returned from grand or humble adventures.

Zanele was waiting near the well when they arrived, her face a mix of relief and curiosity. "You all came back in one piece," she said briskly, though her eyes warmed. "Did you find what you needed?"

Niya and Mandla launched into excited explanations about mechanical parts and new bargains, while Naledi slipped past them, flute still tucked under her arm. She made straight for the Great Tree, drawn by an urge to test her newly repaired instrument in the place that felt most like home.

Beneath the tree's leafy canopy, the evening air felt almost hushed, except for a few crickets tuning up for the night. Naledi took a deep breath, remembering the tune her father had started. She positioned the flute the way the woman had shown her, closed her eyes, and let the notes flow. The opening was tentative, but soon the melody swelled, gathering confidence as each breath formed a vibrant tone. The half-remembered lull turned into a graceful arc, and though she hadn't fully decided on an ending, she found herself improvising, letting the final note linger like a question left hanging in the twilight.

When she opened her eyes, she found Boikonyo standing a few paces away, arms folded, his face unreadable. A flutter of nerves coursed through her. "I; didn't see you," she managed to say.

Boikonyo shrugged, stepping closer. "Didn't want to interrupt." He paused, glancing at the flute. "Sounds better than it used to. Less like a broken whistle, anyway."

Naledi felt her cheeks warm, but she mustered a small smile. "Yeah. Got it fixed in the town. Some nice folks helped me."

He nodded, gaze drifting momentarily to the top of the Great Tree, as if contemplating something bigger than he was ready to voice. "Don't keep me awake with all that playing," he grumbled without real bite, then turned on his heel and left.

Naledi watched him go, a curious mixture of relief and something softer swirling in her chest. Boikonyo's words weren't exactly praise, but they were close enough to acceptance to give her hope.

As dusk settled, painting the sky in gentle purples and pinks, Naledi sank to the ground, the flute resting in her lap. The day's events tumbled through her mind: the bustling market, Mandla's triumphant part for the water pump, Niya's bartering victories, and that kind woman who had coaxed her flute back to life. She felt like the boundaries of her world had stretched, letting in new possibilities and half-formed melodies awaiting their moment to be fully heard.

She pressed her back against the Great Tree's sturdy trunk, gazing at the first stars winking into view. A quiet thought rose in her mind, clear and insistent:

> *How many other instruments lie cracked and voiceless, waiting for a gentle hand? How many broken tunes can still find their way to life?*

It was a question without an easy answer, but it pulsed with a gentle, hopeful chord. Naledi closed her eyes, letting the hush of the village night cradle her. For now, it was enough to know she'd taken another step down this musical path; one that might yet lead her, and perhaps the entire village, to discover that broken things aren't the end of the story. They're an invitation to fix, to learn, and to find a new song worth sharing.

THE RETURN'S RECKONING

The journey home stretched out before them, a red-dust road meandering through tall grasses and solitary baobabs, under a sun that burned hot yet steady. At first, the three travelers;Naledi, Niya, and Mandla;walked as though the world were new-minted and inviting. Their conversation swirled with excited talk of the bustling market they'd left behind: Mandla proudly recounted how he'd bartered for a rare metal valve rumored to salvage the village's creaky water pump, Niya described her clever haggle that saved them a few coins on cloth, and Naledi was still half-dazed with happiness at her newly mended flute.

Every so often, Niya would burst into laughter, recalling a flamboyant vendor or a stray goat that nearly gobbled her bag of roasted nuts. Mandla, quieter by nature, nodded in agreement, but the curve of his lips betrayed his pleasure at the day's success. Naledi, flute cradled beneath her arm, let the sweet memory of the traveling musician's patient repairs play through her mind like a half-remembered lullaby. She kept thinking: *Finally, the flute can sing Father's tune in earnest.*

But as the hours wore on and their village came into view across the last ridge, an uneasy hush settled over them;like a sudden shift in the wind that heralds a coming storm. The huts were there, yes, and the Great Tree rose in the distance as always, its wide canopy distinct against the sky. Yet something felt off, as though the land itself held its breath. Naledi sensed it first;a tightening in her chest that spread to her limbs. By the time they drew close enough to see the figures clustered near the tree's trunk, her heart was thumping in her ears like a warning drum.

"What... what's going on?" Niya asked softly, her voice stripped of the carefree lilt it held mere moments before.

"Surveyors," Mandla muttered, his brow furrowing. There, around the base of the Great Tree, men in crisp uniforms busied themselves with bright-colored flags and silver tools that glinted in the late-afternoon sun. Their movements were measured, methodical;like they were dissecting a piece of land rather than standing at the heart of someone's home.

Naledi's grip on her flute tightened until her knuckles hurt. Each bright flag jabbed into the earth felt like a small insult, as if they were impaling the soil that had sheltered her family for generations. She swallowed a sudden lump in her throat. *No*, she thought, *not this tree... not now.*

Without a word, the three quickened their steps, shoulders tensing. The hum of conversation rose from the small crowd of villagers gathered near the tree, their tones hushed and worried. That was trouble enough. But the sight that truly made Naledi's stomach twist was a single man with a clipboard, scribbling as though pen lines could decide the tree's fate. The men in uniforms seemed unhurried but utterly certain, like they owned the ground beneath their boots and had little regard for what the village might think.

Naledi and her friends stumbled to a stop at the edge of the gathering. Niya's eyes darted among the worried faces;Mama Lindiwe, Ms. Dlamini, a handful of elders from distant huts. Mandla clenched his jaw, the earlier pride on his face gone, replaced by anger and something akin to heartbreak.

"Mama Lindiwe," Naledi called quietly, spotting the old woman leaning on her cane. "What... what is this?"

Mama Lindiwe turned, relief and sadness mingling in her gaze. "Oh, children," she said, her voice grave. "I hoped you wouldn't come home to find this mess. The city men arrived this morning;surveyors, they say, for a government project. Something about clearing the land for a new road or an expansion. They want to mark the tree for removal."

Naledi's mind reeled. She remembered the traveling musician's warm words about how music could bring people together, and now here stood a cold, methodical force that threatened to undo everything her family held dear. She felt her chest constrict. "But the tree... it's part of us," she murmured, tears needling at her eyes. "It's not just wood."

Mama Lindiwe pressed her thin lips into a line, her weathered hands trembling against her cane. "They offered compensation to the village," she said, her tone edged with bitterness. "Some folks think it's a fair price; others can't stand the idea of losing our heart."

A harsh laugh rang out behind them. Naledi spun to see Boikonyo, arms folded as though to ward off any protest. His face carried that mix of tension and regret she'd come to recognize in him, though anger flared in his eyes as well.

"You should've stayed," he snapped, directing his words at Naledi. "This is no time for wandering off to markets."

Mandla stepped forward, bristling at the accusation. "We weren't wandering for fun, Boikonyo. We found a part that could save the water pump;something this village sorely needs. Meanwhile, these strangers are trying to uproot our tree."

Naledi cringed at the bitterness in her brother's gaze. "Why didn't you send word?" she asked, voice trembling. "We would have come back sooner."

"There was no time," Boikonyo replied, his posture rigid. "They showed up unannounced, carrying their flags and documents. I tried talking sense into them, but they have city orders. And some in the village want the money more than they want this tree."

Naledi felt a spike of panic, or maybe heartbreak. "But this tree… it's our heritage. Father cherished it. Are we just giving it up for a handful of coins?"

Boikonyo's jaw tightened. "Progress doesn't care about heritage. You think your music will stop them from cutting it down?"

Her flute felt suddenly heavy, as though each note it could produce weighed a hundred pounds. Naledi swallowed, tears stinging her eyes. "Maybe not, but we have to try."

Boikonyo stared at her a moment, pain flickering across his face. Then he shook his head. "This village can't live on memories and dreams. That tree's old. If it has to go so the rest of us can move forward, maybe that's the price." He turned away, leaving Naledi pinned between anger and sorrow.

That evening, the tension weighed on every corner of the village like an invisible storm cloud. Where folks might ordinarily gather to chat over goat's milk or trade small jokes about the day's chores, now they spoke in hushed murmurs, glancing worriedly at the Great Tree's looming shape. Some older residents scowled at the sight of surveyor flags dotting the roots, while a few younger men tapped their chins, wondering if new roads might bring more business or job opportunities.

Naledi huddled with Niya and Mandla outside her hut, the air thick with worry. Mandla recounted how he'd tried to speak with one of the surveyors, only to be dismissed as though he were a curious child. Niya muttered that she'd confronted a villager who supported cutting the tree for compensation, nearly losing her temper at his stubbornness.

At last, Mandla sighed, running a hand over his face. "I hate to say it, but Boikonyo might be right. How can we fight city orders? They have official documents, laws... things we can't just wave away."

Naledi's chin lifted. "There must be something we can do," she said, setting the flute in her lap. "We can't just stand by and let them tear it down."

Niya looked at her friend's determined expression. "What are you thinking?"

Naledi hesitated, fingers drumming lightly on the flute's smooth surface. She pictured her father, remembered his half-finished tune and the musician's gentle words: *Music is a bridge;something that can move hearts when words fail.* Could the villagers be reminded of the tree's significance if they felt it, not just heard facts?

"I'm thinking... I'll play," she said softly, voice trembling with emotion. "I'll gather everyone I can under the tree, show them how it once saved us, how it's our story. Father's melody might remind them that this isn't just a patch of land, but our home."

Mandla rubbed his chin thoughtfully. "Music might sway them, yes. Mama Lindiwe's told us enough stories about how the tree united the village in hard times. Perhaps a new tune can do the same."

Niya nodded, eyes bright with the spark of a plan. "We'll invite everyone;those who favor cutting the tree, those who don't, and especially the ones on the fence. Let them see that our heritage isn't up for sale. Maybe that's enough to shift minds."

A breeze ruffled the sparse grass at their feet, carrying the faint rustle of night insects. Naledi gazed at the Great Tree's silhouette, towering over huts that now seemed small and fragile. "I'll do it tomorrow," she whispered, as though speaking to both the tree and herself. "I'll play for them."

The night brought little sleep to Naledi's home. She kept tossing on her mat, images flitting through her mind of city men hacking at the tree while her flute notes fell on deaf ears. Now and then, she heard Boikonyo pacing outside, as though he too wrestled with dilemmas he'd rather not face. Zanele murmured in her sleep, her words jumbled but worried, as if the threat to the tree weighed on her dreams.

Naledi rose once near midnight, stepping outside. The moon cast a gentle glow across the huts, and the Great Tree's leaves rustled softly, as if beckoning her. She found herself walking to it, pressing a palm against its ancient bark. A wave of sadness swelled in her chest. The thought of losing this living testament to her father's stories, to the village's roots, felt like losing a piece of herself.

She lifted the flute to her lips, letting a quiet melody flow;a whisper in the moonlight, carrying the sorrow and the steely resolve mingling in her heart. It was a near-silent concert, for nobody's ears but hers and the tree's, but it steadied her. She remembered how the traveling musician had said each note comes from the breath of life, how a well-played tune can speak deeper than words. She hoped, come dawn, that would hold true for her neighbors.

By morning, the weather had shifted ominously, a cluster of gray-blue clouds forming on the horizon. It felt like nature mirrored the village's mood;uncertain, restless, ready to unleash a storm. Still, Naledi rose with purpose. Niya and Mandla knocked on her door early, their expressions tense but supportive.

"Are you sure you want to do this?" Mandla asked. "What if no one listens?"

Naledi glanced down at the flute in her hands, feeling its weight but also its potential. "People will listen," she said softly, "because they have to. This is our home, and we can't give it up without a fight."

Niya squeezed Naledi's shoulder, offering a faint, hopeful smile. "Then let's gather them."

They split up, knocking on doors, coaxing folks out with the promise of a village meeting. Some responded with weary shrugs, others with sparks of curiosity. By the time a soft drizzle began to fall, they'd rounded up a fair gathering under the Great Tree;some standing with arms crossed, some leaning on walking sticks, and a few children perched on the tree's massive roots, eyes gleaming with curiosity. A handful of the surveyors were there too, eyeing the proceedings with mild disinterest, clipboards still in hand.

At the center of it all, Naledi felt her pulse hammering. She stood beneath the broad trunk, Niya and Mandla at her sides, Boikonyo lurking near the back, and Zanele offering a subtle nod of encouragement from across the circle. The drizzle picked up, pattering on leaves overhead, but no one moved away. The tension was thick as a rope.

Naledi raised the flute, inhaling so deeply she thought her lungs might burst. For a split second, she feared no sound would emerge;but as she exhaled, a single clear note cut through the damp air. She followed it with another, forming the start of her father's tune, the notes she'd pieced together with so much effort and hope. The tree seemed to resonate with the melody, each leaf trembling as though in gentle applause.

Slowly, the villagers quieted, eyes drawn to Naledi as the tune swelled. She poured everything she had into that music;the memory of Father humming behind the huts at dusk, the traveling musician's gentle wisdom, the sense of home she found under these very branches. She let the melody rise, painting sorrow, then shift into something brighter, testifying to the resilience that had always bound them. When she reached the final note, she willed it to linger, a plea to the hearts of everyone standing in the drizzle.

When the last echo faded, the hush that followed felt profound. Raindrops pinged on leaves, a soft drumming that filled the silence. Naledi lowered the flute, tears mingling with raindrops on her cheeks. She looked around, seeing confusion, wonder, a few awed faces, and in some, the glimmer of a softened resolve.

Then Mama Lindiwe stepped forward, leaning heavily on her cane. Her voice trembled but carried conviction. "We have roots here," she said, nodding at Naledi. "This tree saved us once, and it has stood over every joy and sorrow we've known. Can we truly sell that for a handful of coins?"

A low murmur swept the crowd. Boikonyo shifted uncomfortably, but for once, he didn't speak. One of the surveyors opened his mouth as though to interject, then seemed to think better of it. The light rain continued, each drop a gentle reminder that nature, too, had a voice in this matter.

Naledi felt her chest loosen. The tension was far from gone, but something had changed;like a door cracked open. *Maybe*, she thought, *just maybe, they would find a way to protect the tree after all.* She cradled her flute, heart beating in time with the soft thrumming of raindrops on leaves.

Yet as she looked from face to face;some hopeful, some unconvinced;she knew this was only the beginning of the fight. A half-hour from now, the surveyors might hoist their flags again and speak of official documents. Neighbors might resume bickering over the money. The path to saving the Great Tree would be neither short nor simple.

But at least, she reminded herself, she'd found her voice;and the tree had heard it, as had the village. She let the drizzle wash over her, the flute a comforting presence against her side. *Music might not solve everything*, she thought, *but it can open hearts.* And sometimes, opening hearts is the first step to turning a quiet storm of doubt into a chorus of unity.

Standing there under the gathering gray sky, Naledi felt the storm's electricity dance around them. It was a storm of arguments, of old wounds and new possibilities, all swirling in the damp air. But perhaps, with a little courage, a little music, and the bonds that had always connected them, they would weather this storm as they had so many before;holding fast to their roots, ready to grow toward whatever dawn awaited next.

ONE TUNE, ONE HEART

Late-afternoon sunshine draped the village square in a warm, golden haze, painting each hut with a gentle glow. Yet beneath that lazy glow lay a tension you could feel in the air;like a hush that settles just before a storm, or maybe the moment when the world decides to hold its breath.

Naledi stood at the periphery of this stillness, her recently mended flute cradled in her hands. She thought her heart might vault from her ribcage, so strong was its thudding. It didn't help that the Great Tree loomed behind her, ancient and watchful, its leafy branches stirring in a breeze that seemed to whisper, *Go on, child.*

Just then, Niya popped around the corner, her bright smile as steadfast as a sunrise. "I told Ms. Dlamini about tonight," she announced, planting her hands on her hips with a look of triumph. "She said she'd drop by after her evening cup of tea. Mama Lindiwe's on her way, too;can you believe she's bringing that old drum?"

Naledi's chest fluttered with something akin to hope. "And Mandla?" she asked, her voice quivering despite her best effort to sound calm.

"He's coming," Niya said, eyes dancing with mischief. "He had to charm Boikonyo first, though, something about fences needing mending before sundown. You know how your brother is."

A soft chuckle escaped Naledi's lips, though her nerves still felt like a tightly wound string. Boikonyo had been in a strange mood since they'd returned from their trip;part scolding them for running off, part begrudgingly pleased at the water pump's improvement. As for the flute, well, his eyes tended to narrow whenever she raised it, but that hadn't stopped her from pressing on.

Sure enough, heavier footsteps announced Boikonyo's approach. He rounded the corner, shadow stretching along the dusty path, with Mandla trailing just behind;one hand raised in apology. "Told him it was important," Mandla murmured. "He took some convincing."

Boikonyo folded his arms across his chest, mouth slanted in a skeptical frown. "You really mean to play that flute here in front of everybody?"

Naledi forced a swallow, her voice quavering only a little. "Yes," she managed. "It's not just about the flute. It's about everything;this tree, the village, all we've been through. If people hear the melody, maybe they'll remember what we're trying to protect."

Her brother considered her words for a moment, the afternoon light catching the tight line of his jaw. Finally, he shrugged. "Fine," he said. "Just don't embarrass yourself." He stalked away, arms still crossed, but the bite in his words didn't feel quite as sharp as it used to.

Little by little, people trickled into the Great Tree's clearing, drawn by curious whispers and the promise of something unusual. Mama Lindiwe arrived soon after, her drum slung beneath one arm and her cane tapping the ground with each measured step. She nodded to Naledi in silent encouragement. Ms. Dlamini followed with a basket of freshly baked rolls, explaining with a smile that "no village gathering should leave a body hungry." Even Boikonyo lingered at the edge of the clearing;arms folded, yes, but notably present.

Naledi's palms felt damp as she stepped forward, flute held tight to her chest. Only fifteen or twenty villagers had gathered;by no means the entire community;but they seemed to represent all corners of the village. In that moment, it felt like every eye was upon her. The Great Tree cast a long shadow across the packed earth, its leaves rustling in the faint breeze. Niya slipped behind Naledi and gave her a nudge so gentle it was almost a whisper: "Go on. They're waiting."

Naledi cleared her throat. The crowd quieted. She tried to speak, finding her voice shakier than expected. "I; wanted to share a melody," she began, letting her gaze sweep across the expectant faces. "One my father started long ago, but never finished. With help from Niya, Mandla, and… from the tree," she added in a softer tone, "I've been trying to piece it together. I hope it reminds us of what we stand to lose if we give up on this place;on ourselves."

She raised the flute, drew a breath that felt half-hope, half-terror, and let the first note flow. It was tentative, quivering at the edges, but she pressed on. The melody unfolded in gentle arcs, drifting around the clearing like morning mist. Naledi pictured her father's face, the way he might have hummed a half-tune by the huts, and she added her own embellishments;a brief trill here, a pause there;making it as much her song as it was his.

When she reached the place he'd left unfinished, she recalled the words of the old merchant who'd repaired her flute: *Let it rise.* So she did;took the melody soaring upward in a triumphant climb, then let it descend into a delicate, wistful hush that reminded her of dusk under the Great Tree. The final note lingered in the warm air, drifting into the hush of rustling leaves.

For an instant, no one spoke. The silence was profound, weighty, like they'd all recognized something deeper than words. Then Mama Lindiwe, eyes glistening with unshed tears, rapped her drum with a soft, steady beat. "That," she said, her voice hushed but resonant, "is the sound of our roots."

Like a ripple in a pond, the crowd stirred. A few tentative claps sparked here and there, growing into a heartfelt applause. Ms. Dlamini approached, cheeks shining. "Naledi," she said, her voice trembling, "thank you for reminding us. We almost forgot how much this tree;and our history;matter."

The applause faded, replaced by a sense of reverent curiosity. People lingered longer than they might have on an ordinary evening, exchanging quiet words about the village's past and the tree's role in it. Some said they were willing to reconsider the idea of letting outsiders tear it down. Others patted Naledi's arm with admiration, as if her flute had bridged a gap they hadn't realized existed.

Mama Lindiwe, drum at her side, beckoned Naledi over. The old woman's expression brimmed with both fondness and relief. "Child," she said, voice low so only Naledi could hear, "that tune of yours ain't just music; t's a call to remember who we are."

Naledi swallowed, her heart still pounding from the performance. "I wanted them to feel what I felt," she said. "I'm not even sure if that's possible, but;"

Mama Lindiwe offered a knowing chuckle, patting her drum's worn surface. "You did more than that. You stirred the roots. Now we'll see if the branches can hold."

At that moment, Boikonyo stepped out of the shadows, crossing the clearing toward Naledi. His arms were still folded, but the tightness in his posture looked eased. For a second, Naledi tensed;half expecting a rebuke. Instead, he nodded once, reluctantly but sincerely. "You played well," he said, a faint crease of warmth on his brow. "Maybe... maybe it's not such a waste of time."

A rush of gratitude filled Naledi, so strong she could scarcely speak. She managed a small, shaky smile. "Thank you, Boikonyo."

That night, the air in the village felt lighter, as if some invisible burden had been lifted. Folks still wore their worries;surveyors' flags weren't magically disappearing;but something akin to hope flickered in every conversation. Niya and Mandla broke out the last of Ms. Dlamini's rolls, savoring them under the tree's canopy while day gave way to twilight. Boikonyo even stuck around, pacing near the edge of the clearing but not objecting to the soft chatter.

"Think this'll change minds?" Niya asked, her tone quieter than usual.

Naledi gazed at the tree, its branches illuminated by a handful of lanterns villagers had strung up earlier. "I'm not sure," she admitted. "But it's a start."

Mandla nodded thoughtfully, the last bit of roll in his hand forgotten. "Sometimes, all it takes is a small note to begin a bigger song, right?"

Naledi let the words wash over her, drawing the flute back into her lap. She thought of how, just a day ago, she'd walked this path burdened by fear;fear that her melody might be too fragile to sway a single soul. Yet here she was, having played her heart out beneath the Great Tree's sheltering boughs, feeling that perhaps;just perhaps;she'd kindled a spark that could grow into a flame of unity.

A hush settled as the evening crickets began their nightly chorus. Naledi raised her flute again, this time not in a grand performance, but as a quiet offering to the dusk. She played a soft tune, something improvised that blended the lullaby-like sweetness of her father's melody with the new strength she'd gained. Niya and Mandla listened in serene appreciation, while Boikonyo paused his pacing to cast an unreadable glance her way.

When the notes faded, Naledi felt the hush again;gentler now, not the tense silence of before, but a calm that said *Yes, we're still here, and we still believe.* She rested her back against the tree's trunk, letting the lantern light reveal the determination in her friends' eyes.

She breathed in, then let her thoughts roam. *What if every person carries a tune;some part of them that speaks to the world if only they dare to let it out? And what if the difference between saving a tree and losing it is someone's willingness to share that tune?*

In the gathering darkness, she couldn't see the surveyors' flags, nor their stern faces, but she knew they remained. Tomorrow, or perhaps the day after, the men with clipboards and measuring tapes would return, armed with official documents. Yet for tonight, the village had reclaimed this clearing as a place of unity, anchored by an old tree and a girl's melody that had bridged the gap between fear and memory.

Niya rested her head on Mandla's shoulder, eyes drifting shut. Mandla rummaged through his tool bag, half-distracted, content to bask in the moment. Naledi, flute warm in her hands, closed her eyes as well. She thought of her father, whose half-finished song she was slowly turning into her own, and felt the comforting pulse of the Great Tree behind her, as though it beat in rhythm with her heart.

She didn't have all the answers, not by a long shot. But she felt certain of one thing: a note played from the heart can awaken deeper truths, and once those truths are stirred, they're not so easily silenced.

And so the question rose in her mind, quiet yet strong:

If music can rouse a village to remember its roots, what else might it kindle when we dare to let it rise?

WHERE ROOTS STAND TALL

Morning arrived clothed in a stillness so tense it felt as though the earth had paused for breath. Over the modest village of twelve huts, the sun rose with a cautious light, sending beams through tattered clouds and casting elongated shadows across the ground. At first glance, everything looked the way it always did; goats ambling by, a woman or two tending early chores, the Great Tree's branches brushing the dawn sky. But Naledi sensed that something was off, like a tune played a fraction sharp. She woke with a start, her ears pricked by unfamiliar voices, urgent and sharp as broken glass.

The surveyors, they must've come at last. The words rattled around her head like stones. She sat upright on her sleeping mat, reaching automatically for her flute. It was cradled beside her, the polished wood gleaming faintly in the dim interior. No time to think; she gathered it close, stepping carefully past Zanele, who stirred in her sleep but did not wake. Slipping outside felt like diving into a dream; one of those unsettling ones where the air carries a warning you can't quite name.

The village center was alive with tension. Men in trim uniforms clustered near the Great Tree, conferring among themselves as though deciding the land's fate could be accomplished with crisp notes on a clipboard. Brightly painted bulldozers and trucks loomed behind them, their metal flanks reflecting the early sunlight in glints that stung the eye. Around these intruders stood the villagers, voices low and fearful, as though each person teetered between anger and apprehension.

Naledi gripped her flute so hard her knuckles ached. *Not the tree,* she thought. *They can't just show up and destroy what's ours.* Her stomach twisted, fear mingling with the lingering echoes of last night's hope.

She spotted Boikonyo at the forefront, shoulders set like stone. "You can't simply march in here and take what belongs to us," he was saying, his tone carrying the assertiveness he often reserved for family quarrels. "This tree has been here longer than we have records for;longer than your papers or fancy machines can imagine."

The man standing opposite Boikonyo had the stiff posture of a fencepost and the bored look of someone who'd rather be somewhere else. "We're not here to debate heritage," he replied flatly, tapping a pencil against his clipboard. "This land's been surveyed for development. Compensation has been arranged for those involved."

That word;*compensation*;sent a shiver through the crowd. Mama Lindiwe, leaning on her old cane with knuckles as pale as her hair, spoke up, her voice wavering with suppressed rage. "You can't compensate a people's soul. This tree is our memory. It's borne witness to our births and our burials, our celebrations and our storms. You cut it down, you cut out our heart."

Her words rippled through the villagers, emboldening some, leaving others just as tense. Naledi took a few steps forward, breath ragged. There, near the crowd's edge, Niya and Mandla hovered, concern etched on their faces. Mandla caught her eye, giving a small nod that said, *We stand together.* Yet his set jaw betrayed his own fear. Niya's gaze flicked between the surveyors' machinery and the tree, her fists balled in silent frustration.

The tension grew, voices rising, but the men with clipboards and measuring tapes simply looked on, impassive. Boikonyo, for all his bold words, faltered. His shoulders slumped a fraction, as though the weight of unstoppable progress pressed down on him. The bulldozers and trucks behind the officials gleamed like misplaced gods of steel, oblivious to the heartbreak they promised.

Naledi felt something stir in her chest. She had no grand plan, but she did have the flute under her arm; a bridge between memory and hope. *Maybe,* she thought, *music won't solve everything, but I can try.* Before she had time to second-guess herself, her feet carried her to the base of the Great Tree. The crowd parted in confusion, heads turning to follow her small figure as she stepped clear of the throng.

She swallowed hard. The hush that fell was immediate, and in it she heard her own pulse hammering. Somewhere behind her, Boikonyo watched in stunned silence, uncertainty etched on his face. The surveyors looked puzzled, their fancy pens and measuring tapes hanging in midair.

Naledi drew a breath so deep it felt like she inhaled the whole morning sky. "Before you decide the worth of this tree," she called, voice trembling but determined, "I want to show you what it means."

And with that, she lifted the flute to her lips and began to play.

The first note was soft, tentative; like a dawn bird testing whether it was safe to sing. But the second note swelled, carrying more confidence, until the melody flowed in delicate arcs around the clearing. This was her father's half-finished tune, resurrected and expanded by her own longing. In it lived the laughter of children playing tag under these branches, the hum of family gatherings when storms pounded the huts, the hush of dawn prayers after a bad harvest. Each trill spoke of belonging, each pause of the quiet moments that bond a community into something stronger than any blueprint or plan.

She let the melody climb higher, weaving in the bright flare of hope she'd learned from the traveling musician: *Let it rise.* The final phrase soared, then dipped into a gentle ending that felt like a gentle reminder that, after all is said and done, they're still neighbors bound by more than coins or titles.

When the last note died away, the clearing held its breath. Even the trucks and bulldozers seemed halted, as though the trees and the machines had called a brief truce. The men in uniforms stood frozen, some blinking as if waking from a dream. And the villagers looked at Naledi;and at one another;with an emotion that verged on reverence.

Naledi lowered the flute, hands shaking. "This tree isn't just wood," she said, voice unsteady yet insistent. "It's our story;ours. You can't buy or sell it like a sack of grain."

In the hush that followed, Mama Lindiwe struck her drum in a low, resonant beat, one that seemed to rise from the earth itself. Slowly, neighbors joined in;clapping, stamping feet, tapping makeshift sticks against the ground. The rhythm grew, a communal heartbeat that left no ear untouched. It was defiance and history and hope, all bound into a single, throbbing pulse.

The surveyors exchanged uneasy glances, their assumed authority wilting. The man with the clipboard cleared his throat. "We... we'll need to consult further before any final action," he said at last, words stumbling from a face now stripped of smug certainty. He gestured to his team, and one by one, they withdrew, the bulldozers reversing with a low mechanical rumble that seemed almost embarrassed by its own intrusion.

A whoop of relief exploded from the villagers. Naledi stood there, breathless, as Niya and Mandla barrelled into her for a fierce hug. She felt her flute pressed between them, warm against her heart. Even Boikonyo approached with a faint nod, an unusual mixture of pride and humility lighting his face. "You've got courage, little sister," he said quietly. "More than I ever gave you credit for."

Naledi's cheeks warmed, tears pricking at the corners of her eyes. "It wasn't just me," she managed to say. "It was all of us. And the tree, too."

Boikonyo cast a glance upward at the massive canopy. For a moment, his stiff posture softened. "Maybe you're right," he admitted, voice low.

That evening, the village gathered beneath the Great Tree, a bright fire crackling at its base. It was as though the morning's crisis had welded everyone together more tightly. Children ran about laughing, and grown-ups lingered over shared memories of how the tree sheltered them in times of need. Mama Lindiwe's drum led a patchwork of voices in old songs, their echoes dancing among the branches.

Naledi sat with her flute cradled in her lap, the firelight flickering across her face. Zanele settled beside her, eyes tender. "Your father would've beamed with pride today," she said, resting a hand on Naledi's shoulder. "He always hoped music could hold us together."

Naledi let out a trembling breath. "Maybe it can," she whispered, recalling the surge of unity that her simple tune had evoked.

Zanele nodded. "It already has."

They gazed up into the starlit canopy, the flicker of flame revealing the ragged surveyor flags half-hidden in the dark, evidence that this battle wasn't fully over. Yet for now, there was victory in the air;an assurance that, when the village stood together under the tree's protective shadow, their bonds were stronger than any push for "progress" could sever.

Quietly, Naledi lifted her flute again, joining Mama Lindiwe's drumming in a gentle reprise of her father's melody. The surrounding chatter softened as neighbors paused to listen, some even humming along where they caught the tune's drift. In that moment, she felt the Great Tree's roots anchoring not just the soil, but the entire village's spirit, as if whispering *Stay steadfast. You belong here.*

And in the hush that followed, Naledi believed it too. They would stand strong;tree, village, and melody woven together, daring the world to forget the power of a few simple notes breathed into the stillness of dawn.

RESONANCE OF OLD DREAMS

Dawn arrived in the quietest fashion that morning, as though it were a shy guest unsure of its welcome. A pale gold light brushed the edges of the horizon, revealing the village in soft hues of gray and yellow. It might have been any other day;but for Naledi, it felt like standing in the hush that follows a grand triumph. The Great Tree still rose tall, its branches swaying gently, yet there was a certain question in its rustle, as though waiting for something unspoken. We've saved the tree for now, Naledi thought, but is that all there is to do?

She woke feeling both proud and unsettled. The previous day's victory over the surveyors rang hollow in the morning stillness, like a half-finished melody. She heard faint voices from the cooking area;her brother Boikonyo, in low conversation with Zanele. Words drifted in and out: *land, responsibilities, father.* At that last mention, Naledi felt a knot form in her chest. *Father.* It was rare for his name to be spoken so directly. She paused, breath held, but the conversation dropped to murmurs, leaving her only with echoes.

Later, Naledi found herself drawn toward the Great Tree as a moth is drawn to a flame; irresistibly, and with a sense that something there waited for her. She walked slowly, the flute from yesterday's performance cradled against her side. One hand brushed a low-hanging branch, as if seeking comfort. She could almost sense the tree's steady, ancient presence returning the gesture: *I'm still here; are you?*

Her mind whirled with questions: *Could the tree truly remain safe if the city insisted on progress? Would yesterday's music be enough to hold back the ambitions of men with clipboards and machines? Or was all their effort just a brief lull before the next wave?* She tried to let the hush of the morning calm her, but the doubts remained.

A voice broke her thoughts like a pebble tossed into still water. "You spend a lot of time here, Naledi." She turned to find Boikonyo standing a few steps away, hands shoved in his pockets. He sounded neither accusatory nor mocking; more like an older brother trying to puzzle out a sibling's strange habits.

Naledi shrugged, hugging the flute close. "It's not just a tree, Boikonyo," she said softly. "We nearly lost it, and I… well, I just want to be sure it's really safe."

He sighed, his gaze drifting to the massive trunk, gnarled with age. "Maybe," he allowed. "But it can't put food on the table or keep the roof from leaking." He paused, voice tinged with weariness. "It never did."

Naledi's heart squeezed. "It doesn't have to be one or the other," she said, her tone catching a faint edge of frustration. "We need practical things, sure, but we also need something that reminds us of why life matters in the first place."

Boikonyo's face twisted in a mirthless grin. "You sound like him, you know."

Naledi blinked. "Like who?"

He ran a hand over his hair, exhaling as though releasing a heavy burden. "Father," he said, letting the word hang in the space between them. "He was the same way; always talking about what wasn't strictly practical but was still worth fighting for."

Naledi's breath caught. They rarely spoke of Father so plainly. "Why don't you ever tell me about him? I remember so little;just glimpses. He whistled sometimes, right? But you were older. You must know more."

For a moment, Boikonyo hesitated, the rigid set of his shoulders loosening. Then, with a small grunt, he sank onto one of the Great Tree's thick roots, elbows on his knees. "It's not easy, Naledi," he said, voice quieter than she'd ever heard it. "Talking about him won't bring him back. And I used to think maybe it was his dreams that pulled him away."

Tentatively, Naledi settled beside him, the rough bark of the root pressing against her legs. "You blamed him for leaving?"

He shook his head slowly, a half-conflicted motion. "I did. But maybe it wasn't just dreams. Maybe… he thought we'd be better off without him." His voice wavered at that last part, as if it pained him to consider.

Naledi swallowed the lump rising in her throat. "He was different, you said. How?"

Boikonyo's eyes flicked to the canopy above, and for a moment he looked younger than his burdens made him seem. "He saw the world in ways nobody else did. Always fixing things no one else dared to fix. Could patch a roof, mend a tool, or calm a fight if he just stepped in. And he loved music;had this old guitar. Didn't care if people rolled their eyes; he'd play it every night if he could, stringing together tunes about places he never got to see."

Naledi felt her pulse quicken. "I never knew about the guitar. What happened to it?"

He grimaced, eyes clouding. "Mama gave it away after he left. Said she couldn't bear to look at it. It hurt too much."

The weight of those words settled in, thick with regret and longing. Naledi bit her lip. "Do you think he would've stayed if he wasn't a dreamer?"

Boikonyo released a slow breath. "Maybe not. Maybe his dreams were the only things holding him for as long as they did. After a while, I stopped trying to figure it out." He paused, then looked at her with a faint, sad smile. "But one thing I know: he would've been proud of you;this flute, that melody. He always said music brings people together. I thought it was just talk, but seeing what you did yesterday..."

He let the sentence trail off, a brief flicker of awe crossing his features. Naledi's eyes stung with tears she hadn't quite admitted to feeling. "It wasn't just me," she whispered, echoing the thought from the day before. "But thank you, Boikonyo."

A comfortable silence stretched between them, broken only by the rustling of leaves in a gentle breeze. Naledi traced the flute's smooth surface, feeling the residual warmth of the musician's repair. She glanced sideways at her brother, noticing the exhaustion etched in his face;the weariness of a man who'd tried to hold a family together when he, too, had lost someone.

"You ever wonder if saving the tree is enough?" she asked softly. "Even if it stands, the problems that pushed Father away might still remain. This village has needs;real, physical ones."

Boikonyo tilted his head back, letting the sun dapple his face through the foliage. "It's not about one event;surveyors or no surveyors. It's about remembering who we are. That tree's a start. It's a symbol of what ties us together, more than a few coins can buy."

A faint smile tugged at Naledi's lips. *He really is changing,* she thought. *Or maybe just allowing himself to speak the truth he's always known.* She raised the flute then, blowing a gentle tune that meandered between sorrow and hope, a quiet conversation with the morning air. Boikonyo closed his eyes, listening, the smallest curve of a smile gracing his mouth. For a brief, shining moment, Naledi felt they were united;brother and sister, carrying the memory of a father who'd once strummed a battered guitar.

When she finished, Boikonyo rose, dusting off his trousers. "You've got a gift, Naledi," he said, gaze flicking over the flute in her hands. "Don't let anyone;least of all me;make you think otherwise."

She tried to speak, but found no words worth forming. Instead, she nodded, tears of gratitude glimmering. Boikonyo offered her an awkward pat on the shoulder before turning away. "Show Mama that tune sometime," he added over his shoulder. "She misses him more than she says." And then he walked back toward the huts, leaving Naledi to the Great Tree's gentle watch.

That evening, as the sun bled orange across the sky, Naledi sat with Zanele near a small cooking fire. The aroma of simmering stew filled the warm air. Zanele's face bore lines Naledi hadn't fully noticed before;lines of care, perhaps from all the years she'd managed alone.

"Mama," Naledi began, voice trembling with the courage it took to broach the topic. "Did you know Father was so passionate about music? Boikonyo said he had an old guitar and played all the time."

Zanele's stirring spoon froze, and for a moment, the fire crackled in the hush. "Yes," she said softly, voice threaded with emotion. "He'd sing about places he never set foot in, dreams he never chased… or maybe he did chase them, and that's why he left." She swallowed. "Sometimes, I hated that guitar for reminding me of the man we lost."

A spike of sadness shot through Naledi's chest, but it was tempered by understanding. "I'm sorry, Mama. I never got to know him the way Boikonyo did. But… I've been working on a melody I think he would've liked. Will you;would you like to hear it?"

Zanele paused, tears shimmering in her eyes. Then she set the spoon aside and folded her hands. "I would," she said, voice husky. "I would very much."

Naledi took up her flute, feeling its familiar weight, and began to play. She started with the gentle rise of father's old tune, weaving in the new phrases she'd discovered in the last few days;phrases that spoke of her own determination, the power of unity, and the quiet love binding this family together even after so many storms. The notes gathered warmth as they danced above the crackle of the cooking fire, floating into the open air of night like a prayer for solace.

When she finally lowered the flute, Zanele's cheeks glistened with tears. "He would've loved it," she murmured, voice tremulous. "He always believed music could mend broken things, though I never understood how."

Naledi let out a shaky breath. "It mends us," she said gently. "Maybe that's all the healing we need."

A ghost of a smile crossed Zanele's lips, and she reached out to take Naledi's hand. "You've brought him back to us, in your own way. Not just through memory, but through something alive;a melody that belongs to us all."

Naledi squeezed her mother's hand, feeling the last of the day's tension melt away. The sun had set fully now, leaving the sky sprinkled with stars. A hush settled across the yard, though far off she could still hear the chirr of crickets and the low bleat of a goat. Yet in that hush, she sensed a profound sense of release;Father's absence no longer weighed as heavily, for his spirit breathed through the notes she'd played.

She touched the flute's smooth surface, thinking of how it had once been broken, silent. Now, it had found its voice, and in turn, had given a voice to her father's unspoken dreams. That same voice had rallied an entire village to protect a tree that stood for more than mere wood.

Behind her, the Great Tree's silhouette was a dark outline against the shimmering stars, its branches swaying softly in the night breeze. She could almost imagine it whispering: *We endure, and so will you.*

In the soft darkness, Naledi answered its unspoken promise: *Yes, we will. Always.*

A CANOPY OF FUTURES

The late-afternoon sun stretched across the village in gentle arcs, as though the very light wished to linger a while longer. It bathed the huts in a soft glow and caught on the broad leaves of the Great Tree, turning them a lustrous green-gold that shivered in the breeze. For a moment, if one paused to look, it felt as though the tree were dipping its branches in thanks, acknowledging the celebration that had sprung up at its roots.

For indeed, the day had been christened a day of festivity;*a day of deliverance*, some called it. Not so long ago, the Great Tree's future teetered on the brink, threatened by surveyors and talk of progress. But now, the threat had been driven off;or, at least, made to think twice;and in the clearing beneath its mighty trunk, half the village had gathered to mark the occasion. Long tables groaned with platters of fruit and fresh bread. Lanterns dangled from branches overhead like tiny stars, ready to glow once dusk arrived. Children darted in and out, squealing in delight over small games that popped up wherever there was a spare patch of ground.

Near the center of it all, Naledi stood with her flute, the same one she'd fought so hard to repair and learn. She had polished it that morning until its wood gleamed in the sun; a testament to both her father's old dream and her own new resolve. Though the scene around her buzzed with laughter and chatter, she felt a warm, calm readiness settle in her chest, a sensation akin to standing on a high bluff and gazing out over a world of endless possibility.

Mandla and Niya bustled about, placing lanterns and organizing a makeshift circle of chairs. "You'll play for us, right?" Mandla called, pausing mid-lantern to grin. "The Tree demands a concert."

Naledi huffed a soft laugh. "Oh, I'll play," she conceded, "but only if you promise not to brag about your water pump triumph in the middle of my performance."

Niya snorted, giving Mandla a friendly elbow. "Hear that? Stay humble, hero."

The sun dipped lower, and as if on cue, the clearing took on a warm glow. Folks who had been drifting in and out suddenly drew closer. Zanele, standing by a row of cooking pots, shared a look with Naledi across the clearing that spoke volumes: pride, gratitude, and a measure of relief that the village had found its footing. Boikonyo arrived a bit later, nodding at a few neighbors, his expression still cautious but considerably softer than the scowl he used to wear. He made his way over to Naledi, arms loosely crossed; more in habit than anger now.

"You ready?" he asked, his voice quiet enough not to carry to the others.

Naledi mustered a smile, feeling a small but persistent flutter in her belly. "Yes, I think so."

He nodded, glancing at the flute. "You've done good, Naledi. Better than I ever expected. If Father could see you, he'd be proud."

Her throat tightened. Words spilled out in a whispered rush: "I hope so. I... I think he'd be proud of all of us."

Boikonyo gave a slight, almost hesitant smile, then melted into the gathering crowd, like a watchful guardian who'd learned new ways to show care. Naledi inhaled slowly, her heart steadying. *Now is the time.*

When the moment finally came, the villagers quieted with a gentle ease, the drums falling silent and the scattered conversations dropping to hush. A circle formed around the base of the Great Tree, the lantern light beginning to flicker overhead as shadows stretched across the dusty ground. Naledi stood at the circle's center, flute raised. Her first note slipped into the night air;quiet at first, as if testing the world's readiness for it. Then came the rest, forming the melody she had pieced together from her father's remnants and her own fresh spirit. The music soared and dipped, carrying in its measures the tale of resilience and the bright promise of tomorrow.

It was more than just a tune. Each phrase spoke of struggles weathered;droughts, storms, and the recent looming threat of men with machines;and of the unbreakable bond between people and the land they called home. The Great Tree had seen every sorrow, every laughter-filled harvest, every child's first steps. Now, under its branches, the villagers found themselves bound anew by the invisible threads of music and memory.

As Naledi played, she sensed the crowd drawing a collective breath, hearts beating in unison. Zanele closed her eyes, hand resting gently over her heart as tears pricked at her lids. Mama Lindiwe, standing with her drum at her side, allowed the tune to wash over her, nodding slowly in time. Even Boikonyo stood near the back, arms uncrossed, his face lit by a quiet, almost wistful smile.

When at last the final note dissolved into the soft night, a silence took hold that felt like the village's very soul had stilled. In that silence lay understanding, gratitude, and something transcendent;a realization that, despite everything, they had held fast. Then the applause began;not just polite clapping, but the sound of a community rejoicing in its own survival: feet stamping, voices cheering, and Mama Lindiwe rapping out a triumphant beat on her drum. Naledi lowered her flute, cheeks flushed, tears welling in the corners of her eyes.

Niya slipped beside her and clasped her hand. "You did it," she murmured, eyes shining. "You brought us all together."

The clearing sparkled with lantern light and laughter as the celebration soared onward. Naledi tucked her flute away, her heart feeling both full and tender as she wove among the villagers. She paused to exchange a grin with Mandla;who, indeed, couldn't resist mentioning the water pump once or twice;and to share a warm hug with Zanele. She locked eyes with Boikonyo for a moment, no words needed; his nod was enough to say *I see you* and *thank you.*

Some time after the drums reached their crescendo and the dancing hit its joyful peak, Naledi found herself back at the base of the tree, leaning against its trunk. The crowd's noise was slightly distant now, a comforting backdrop. She looked up, gazing at the stars glinting through the foliage. For the first time in a long time, the knot in her chest was gone, replaced by a calm knowledge that, while there would always be challenges, they had found the unity to face them.

She thought of her father;the man who once left behind a handful of notes and a dream. In the rustling leaves and the faint echo of music still reverberating in the clearing, she felt him near. *Keep dreaming, Naledi,* she almost heard him say. *Keep creating.* A tear slipped down her cheek, and she smiled, touching the flute. "I will, Papa," she whispered, her voice barely audible beneath the singing wind. "I promise."

Later, when the firelight had dwindled to embers and the villagers were scattered in small, murmuring groups, Naledi sat beneath the Great Tree with Niya and Mandla. The three of them spoke in low tones, occasionally bursting into half-exhausted laughter as they recalled the day's triumph or teased one another about the next big project. In a lull, Mandla nudged Naledi with his elbow and grinned. "So, where do you go from here, famous flute player?"

She laughed softly. "I wish I knew. Maybe we keep doing what we've been doing;fixing what's broken, building what we can. Together."

Niya's eyes glowed in the lanternlight. "And maybe we teach others. Show the village what's possible if we don't give in to doubt."

Naledi leaned her head back against the trunk, gazing up at the layered canopy. "That's what this tree has taught us, isn't it? That some things stand because we believe in them enough to protect them."

The stars overhead seemed to flicker in agreement. In that gentle, welcoming night, the trio felt like they were part of something far greater, a legacy reaching back through the ages to the sapling that once provided water in a drought, to the father who once left behind a half-finished melody for his daughter to discover.

Yes, Naledi thought, a wave of contentment brimming in her chest. They had saved the tree. But the tree had, in turn, saved them; drawing them back to their roots, reminding them of the harmony they could achieve if they only listened to one another. Tomorrow might bring new troubles;men with bigger machines or new dreams that demanded risk. But tonight, they had each other and the gentle reassurance of the Great Tree's silent testimony: *Grow. Hope. Endure.*

And in that shared moment under the starry canopy, it felt both enough and yet also just the beginning.

Printed in Great Britain
by Amazon